AVID

READER

PRESS

The Appointment

(Or, The Story of a Jewish Cock)

Katharina Volckmer

AVID READER PRESS

NEW YORK   LONDON   TORONTO   SYDNEY   NEW DELHI

Avid Reader Press
An Imprint of Simon & Schuster, Inc.
1230 Avenue of the Americas
New York, NY 10020

First Avid Reader Press hardcover edition September 2020

AVID READER PRESS and colophon are trademarks of Simon & Schuster, Inc.

For information about special discounts for bulk purchases,
please contact Simon & Schuster Special Sales at 1-866-506-1949
or business@simonandschuster.com.

The Simon & Schuster Speakers Bureau can bring authors to your
live event. For more information or to book an event, contact the
Simon & Schuster Speakers Bureau at 1-866-248-3049 or visit our
website at www.simonspeakers.com.

Interior design by Carly Loman

Manufactured in the United States of America

10   9   8   7   6   5   4   3   2   1

Library of Congress Cataloging-in-Publication Data has been applied for.

ISBN 978-1-9821-5017-4
ISBN 978-1-9821-5019-8 (ebook)

*In memory of David Miller—in whose chair
I wrote this novel.*

The Appointment

I KNOW THAT THIS MIGHT NOT BE THE BEST MOment to bring this up, Dr. Seligman, but it just came to my mind that I once dreamt that I was Hitler. I feel embarrassed talking about it even now, but I really was him, overlooking a mass of fanatical followers, I delivered a speech from a balcony. Wearing the uniform with the funny, puffy legs, I could feel the little moustache on my upper lip, and my right hand was flying through the air as I mesmerised everyone with my voice. I don't remember exactly what I was talking about—I think it had something to do with Mussolini and some absurd dream of expansion—but that doesn't matter. What is fascism anyway but ideology for its own sake; it carries no message, and in the end the Italians beat us to it. I can't walk for more than a hundred metres in this city without seeing the words *pasta* or *espresso*, and their ghastly flag is hanging from every corner. I never see the word *sauerkraut* anywhere. It was never feasible for us to hold down an empire for a thousand years with our deplorable cuisine; there are limits to what you can impose on people, and anyone would break free after a second serving of what we call food. It was always our weak point, we never created anything that was meant to be enjoyed without a higher purpose—it is not for nothing that there is no word for pleasure in German; we only know lust and joy. Our throats never get wet enough to suck anyone with devotion because we were all raised on too much dry bread. You know that horrible bread we eat and tell everyone about, like some sort of self-perpetuating myth? I think it's a punishment from God for all the crimes we have committed, and forthwith nothing as sensual as a baguette or as moist as the blueberry muffins they serve here will ever come out of that country. It's one of the reasons I had to leave: I no longer wanted to be complicit in the bread lie. But anyway, as I was delivering what we would now have to call a hate speech, I felt that the orgiastic applause coming from beneath me only served as poor compensation for my obvious deformities. I was so painfully aware that I looked nothing like the Aryan ideal I had been going on about for all those years. I mean, I did not have a clubfoot, but still, all of the dead Jews in the world, not even my alleged vegetarianism, would make me eligible for one of those hot Riefenstahl pics. I felt like a fraud. Had no one noticed that I looked like an old potato with plastic hair? I can still feel the sadness I woke up with that day, the sadness of knowing that I would never get to be one of those beautiful blond German boys with their Greek bodies and that skin that turns so wonderfully golden in the sun, the feeling that I would never be what I felt I should have been.

I don't want to say that I felt sorry for Hitler, and it's still not acceptable to wipe out an entire civilisation because you feel unhappy in your body and because they represent what you hate about yourself, but it did make me think about his private life. Hitler's everyday. Have you ever thought about the Führer in his pyjamas, Dr. Seligman, waking up with messy hair, stumbling across the room looking for his slippers? I am sure some sad person has written a book about his domestic life, but I much prefer to imagine it myself; books would only find a way to make it dull. I can see the swastika-themed bedsheets and matching pyjamas, everything down to his breakfast bowl. I saw those once in Poland in one of those weird antique shops entirely dedicated to the memorabilia of their tormentors, where they were selling bowls and plates with tiny swastikas at the bottom. It almost felt like some sort of perverted Barbie universe where if you saved long enough, you could buy a whole new life, shiny and matching. I could even imagine little TV spots with a well-oiled Hitler doll on one of those glittering horses, saving a good German woman from the hands of some leering Jew, riding off into the sunset, the race protected and safe. Savvy as they were when it came to the media, I think the Nazis really missed out on a marketing opportunity there, imagine all the fun little German children could have had with something like a LEGO concentration camp called Freudenstadt—build your own oven, organise your own deportations, and don't forget to conquer enough lebensraum. They could even have gone for an adult line—aside from all the gloves and lampshades made from skin they could have had horse-themed butt plugs made from real enemy hair. But I guess that ship has sailed now. And I don't mean to offend you, Dr. Seligman, especially now that you have your head between my legs, but don't you think that there is something kinky about genocide?

The other day as I was coming home there was a person under the train, someone who wanted to leave with a bang and stick it to some fellow commuters as a final gesture in our modern warfare of despair. And so I had to walk back through one of those parts of London where people from previous generations live, with real furniture and clean bathtubs, with those bright shops for children that make childhood look like it was a French invention and those front gardens where spring seems to arrive earlier than anywhere else. I especially love those dark magnolia blossoms; they look so elegant, almost purple. Have you seen them, Dr. Seligman? No one would ever dream of dumping their rubbish in front of one of those houses—they render even coarse natures delicate—yet my driveway is constantly subject to other people's violations, and I find anything from rusty freezers to old makeup bags and used toys when I peek through my curtains in the morning. I wonder what it is about me that makes others assume that I will rejoice in their broken objects and I have come very close to making my humiliation public and leaving a note asking them to stop, which is almost as bad as asking for food or a clean pair of knickers. Have you ever tried to make someone respect your basic humanity? I am not asking for anything drastic like dignified sex or real emotions; at least leave something fun for me sometimes, but this feels like I am possessed by some twisted fairy who wants to make sure that no prince will ever get to see my window and that all my dreams will eventually smell of fox piss and resemble the kind of plastic you see in documentaries about how we killed Mother Nature. They become objects of guilt and disgust, and at night I try to fall asleep without a clear vision of my future. That's why I have long stopped going to those parts of the city I cannot afford; they make me see all my failures through a magnifying glass and remind me of all the things my parents will never forgive. Why had I not just spread my legs at the right moment, taken better care of my body, and married one of the men with the dark magnolia trees in their front garden? I could have been one of those women in fancy cafés with not a single thing to worry about. It would have been like living in a chocolate shop, Dr. Seligman. I think that's why rich people always look like someone just fucked them with a bespoke strap-on whilst someone else ironed their fresh bedsheets in the room next door. That's also why their children are less ugly—because they can actually afford them, because the children know that they have a right to be there. That must be how superiority works. Do you think it was a mistake to come and see you instead, Dr. Seligman?

I'm not scared of what we are about to do, though, Dr. Seligman. I'm not scared of dying or anything like that. I know that I can trust you, and that death is silent. It's never the loud things that kill us, the things that make us vomit and scream and cry. Those things are just looking for attention. They are like cats in spring, Dr. Seligman—they want to feel our resistance, to wake us up at night and listen to the melody of our curses, but they mean no harm. Death is all that grows inside us, all that will finally burst, leaving its natural circuits and flooding all that needs to breathe. The infections that fester unnoticed, the hearts that break without warning. That's where all those films and TV programmes with their pornographic violence got it wrong, Dr. Seligman: people rarely get killed like that. It's all within us already, the way we are going to die, there is nothing others can do about it—just as from a certain age all the people we are going to hurt and fuck are already walking the planet. I have always found it a strange thought, that our whole life is basically already here. It's just our concept of time that forces us into a linear point of view. But that's why I'm not scared, Dr. Seligman; I can feel that it's not my destiny to die under your hands. They are far too gentle to even leave a scar.

And it's not like I have never been in love, Dr. Seligman. I know that you can't see me very well, but I don't want you to think that I am one of those people without feelings or empathy. It's just that falling in love has never been easy; it was never the predictable exercise it is for most people because my love never corresponded to my reality. Because no love ever survived the image I had of it. Because K didn't know how to handle his words. And so I stayed alone for most of it—so alone, in fact, that I almost did something stupid the other day, something that would have made me look even more ridiculous, and all because I suddenly remembered my broken heart and thought that writing that letter would make fate regret some of its decisions. It is one of my many deformities that

I always think of fate as some dramatic fat person on a chaise longue, stroking a pathetic pet, waiting for their whims to be humoured. And I always think that there's a way to get to them, to influence their decisions by wearing a special earring or not getting on the obvious train. Or by thinking of an extra-special way to commit suicide. It's just my way of denying that nobody hears my thoughts and that most of my life has taken place in a dark void. I know that it makes no difference whether I get up with my right or my left leg, that there is no higher mechanism at work and that I might as well chop off a leg or rub acid on my toothbrush. The person on the chaise longue wouldn't bat an eyelid and would send me on my unremarkable path anyway; they wouldn't even remember my name. Sometimes I can hear them offering grapes to their pathetic pet and I regret that I was born with this ugly human skin. Just imagine being someone's pet, Dr. Seligman; the kind of unconditional love you would inspire. They would do anything for you—they'd leave the radiator on for you in winter even though they can't afford it, and when you'd be sick on their favourite pair of shoes, they would clean it up with a smile. And then, one day, when you couldn't take it anymore, you could run into traffic and get run over in front of their eyes and break their miserable little hearts. But at least that way you wouldn't leave anything behind, except maybe a collar and a few cherished blankets, nothing that couldn't be buried with you somewhere at the back of the garden. There would be no inheritance, nothing that your descendants would need to manage except for their empty nights and those walks that no longer served a purpose. They wouldn't be in my situation, or that of my family, Dr. Seligman. Now that my grandfather is dead, we are left to grapple with the will of an old man who was a stranger to us, and when I saw my mother at the funeral last week, I could tell how upset she was, not just because of the state I was in.

And yet I almost wrote that letter to Mr. Shimada. I know that you can get addicted to sex toys, that if you treat yourself to too many of those free orgasms, you go numb and real interactions become meaningless. But I always wanted a pen pal, Dr. Seligman; I used to reply to those ads as a child, but no one ever got back to me. Those little German children must have sensed that something wasn't right with me even back then, or maybe they just thought I was a paedophile in disguise. Anyway, I really wanted to correspond with Mr. Shimada about his robots, or, to be honest, I wanted to ask him if he would produce one for me. I had seen him on TV talking about the little sex machines he had designed and created, and he seemed so excited about his vision. Like a modern saviour, Jesus with a walking dildo. I know that those robots are designed to fulfil the sexual needs of men, because men are naturally entitled to having their needs fulfilled, but how difficult can it be to build one with an electronic cock instead? You probably think that would be horribly sad, Dr. Seligman—I can almost feel you frowning down there—but he would only need to remodel it a bit, take off the breasts, close one of its holes, and I don't really care too much about the face. Don't you think it would be best if we all had our own individual robots to fuck? Imagine if we were all satisfied and did not have to explain our desires anymore. But then they would probably come up with some stupid reason why male robots are dangerous or why they are not needed because people without cocks can always find someone around the corner. How the people without cocks need to be controlled for the people with cocks not to feel intimidated, because somehow it is a bad thing when men feel intimidated. But my wish is not political, Dr. Seligman; I have long stopped caring about the universal violence affecting my body. I am just tired, and the idea of being able to focus on my desire alone seems like a long-lost dream. To be able to turn my companion off when I have no emotions left.

In the end I didn't have the courage, because I was worried that Mr. Shimada would think I was a freak. I know that he probably receives a lot of weird mail, but the idea of being judged by someone who builds fuckable mannequins at the other end of the world was quite upsetting. And I have never been to Japan and don't even know what the right formalities would be. And if I had tried to explain all my circumstances, how I intended to use my robot, it would have been a very long letter, and he might have been bored to death and never finished it. Or maybe my circumstances are as banal as anyone else's; they must have broken hearts in Japan, don't you think? Thinking about it now, Dr. Seligman, I am sure that Mr. Shimada would understand, and maybe once this is all over I will write to him. I mean, why else would you fuck a piece of plastic if it wasn't to keep your heart safe? I am sure he will come around and build me my little talking cock. Have you ever been intimate with an object, Dr. Seligman? I was always worried about inserting something that runs on electricity into my body, about electrocuting myself down there and being found in the most unfortunate position. Just think of the headlines: single woman with two cats killed by faulty vibrator. What could be more tragic? Are you aware of any such cases? I mean, I know that there are guarantees and that Japan is not China and that they produce everything to a very high standard, but in the past I never dared. Or, to be honest, and since this is a medical examination and this information might be relevant, I never got beyond inserting a banana into my vagina. One of those bananas with very thick skin and those edges that almost look like pulsating veins. I hate to think of it now, but at the time it had turned me on, and it seemed very low risk. The result was disappointing, though. Things got very dry, and after a while I grew tired of my own movements. It was before I knew that you can apply lube to almost anything and finally understood why people are sometimes admitted to hospital with half their living room up their ass. I think that's what loneliness does to people, Dr. Seligman; they forget how to articulate their desires.

I think it's about to start snowing, Dr. Seligman. Those clouds look like they're about to burst, and I could feel that wintry air as I was walking here earlier. You know that moment in the late afternoon when a special kind of grey seems to have become part of the atmosphere, when it's about to swallow the light and it's impossible to distinguish what you see from what you feel? When it's cold enough to see the warmth leaving people's bodies? But on other days you must have such a nice view from up here. Do you ever go and sit in that park outside your window, Dr. Seligman? When I still had a job, I used to go and sit in the park near work during my lunch breaks, the kind of pretty park the Germans would have vandalised but that the Brits treat like a sacred space, with real flowers and well-meaning dogs. But now I don't really go anymore. I fear that people might notice what's going on with me, and sitting there in my current state I would feel like a fraud. The other reason I stopped going to the park was that having to regularly listen to other people's conversations made my organs bleed. Nothing else makes you realise with such brutality how banal life really is. As long as you only talk to yourself, you can gloss over some of the details, but when I am exposed to the mindless chatter of others I'm immediately possessed by a very strong urge to kill myself, as I can no longer ignore the fact that we are nothing but a dying star drifting in an endless void, not deserving any of the sunlight that keeps us alive. If it were up to me, the sun couldn't explode soon enough and put an end to all this raging stupidity. I even contemplated going mute altogether. You might find that hard to imagine, Dr. Seligman, but I just didn't want to be part of the oral pollution anymore. Back when I still used to sit in the park, I always wished for these mindless people to be shat on by pigeons, for them to be marked and stained for the offence they had committed, for not realising that their so-called personalities are nothing but layers of replaceable crap. It's also the only way I could see myself becoming a pigeon lady, imagining all the bread and seeds I'd be feeding my little birds transformed into ugly yellow-brown shit that would land on people's heads, coats, and food. The shit would stop them from producing any more of their dribble, to find, however brief, a moment of silence when all you can hear is their despair and the pigeons' satisfied cooing. Such are my dreams, Dr. Seligman, and if you really think about it, it's these small acts of revenge that make all the difference, and slowly but surely the pigeons are destroying the facades of our most beloved cities with their endless rain of shit. Just think of Notre Dame's gargoyles or those lovely buildings in Venice melting under this natural acid shower, and close by you'll find a little pigeon lady, smiling at yet another victory. Imagine if the Nazis had known. Apparently they did try to train bees, though I don't know for what purpose; maybe to make them sniff out Jews and sting them to death. But then if Hollywood hasn't picked up on it yet, it's probably not true. How else would they have resisted a film with the title *Hitler's Beekeepers* when they have already used up most of the possible Hitler-and titles? Personally, I am still waiting for *Hitler's Nail Clippers* and *The True Story behind Hitler's Haircut*. I am sure, though, that they had carrier pigeons for their stupid coded messages, but I am also sure that they were not aware of the destructive power of bird shit. Superior as always, the Swiss know. I once read somewhere that the city of Zurich hired a man to go through the city and shoot pigeons in daylight. I wonder if that includes the pigeon ladies as sources of unrestrained female agency, officially unfuckable like witches and nuns and therefore too free; do you think the Swiss are capable of such hygiene?

You don't need to be scared of me, though, Dr. Seligman, really. Your assistant told me that you are very thorough and that this would take a while, especially the photos, so I don't want you to worry, because I still think that the reasons for my discharge from work were misconstrued and it's unfair to say that I have anger issues. I was angry that day, of course—it was before I had started taking my hormones—but to get suspended like that when they have no idea what it's like for people like me. And I don't think that threatening to staple a coworker's ear to their desk whilst waving a stapler around can really count as violence. Not with those staplers, anyway. I doubt they have ever tried to staple through human flesh and into a solid desk with one of those stiff little plastic things. I was probably more at risk of losing my eyesight from an errant staple, but of course that didn't matter to them. And you don't need to think that they ever provided us with safety glasses; heaven knows how many casualties will be caused by all that cheap stationery.

But now I don't feel sorry anymore; let them all be poisoned from chewing on those horrible pens that turn all handwriting into a lament. Because the worst thing was not losing my job—in this city you starve either way—but that they made me see a therapist called Jason, for otherwise they would have pressed charges. Can you imagine being serious with a therapist called Jason, Dr. Seligman? A therapist who looked like he might also be called Dave or Pete, who had the kind of face that would adapt to anything, like one of those yoga teachers who smile their way through any atrocity, knowing that the universe is backing their cause. And if the sun could break out of herself and revolve around them, she would. That's why people like Jason think they can forgive all those petty human errors, and that's also why I decided to lie to him.

I had no idea what Jason's background was, but I thought that it would wind him up if I told him about my sexual fixation with our dear Führer and that my inability to ever fulfil my desires had brought about my anger and made me want to staple my colleague's earlobe to the desk. I could not tell him about the true nature of my dreams and all the things that were wrong with my body, and after

a while I really began to enjoy my story. I wanted
to be a writer once, Dr. Seligman, and coming up
with a narrative like that was a beautiful experience.
Toward the end Jason could not wait for our sessions to be over, I could feel it. I guess there's nothing more off-putting than a perversion you don't
share; plus, being stuck in a room with a German
talking themselves into a semi-orgiastic state over
imagining being spanked with the Führer's very
own riding crop also poses a moral issue. Even
though Jason didn't really look like he was willing
to invest any unnecessary emotions, I could tell that
he was suffering. But it wasn't just filth—there were
moments of true intimacy, of that paternal chivalry
we all secretly crave, of doubts and broken promises
and the inevitable end of being left for Eva Braun,
his frumpy secretary named after the ugliest colour.
I described in great detail how I petted the dogs for
the last time before returning all those sweet tokens
of affection and how I managed to smuggle out a
strand of his famous hair hidden in a dirty pair of
nylon stockings and a note, in his own handwriting,
requesting me to wear nothing but one of those Jewish skullcaps. I think Jason actually winced when
I told him how I had been daydreaming about my

little A, that's how I called Hitler by myself, making me say "My name is Sarah" before punishing me with his mighty crop. In my dreams I had very dark hair and a pair of those lovely dark eyes, and everything felt so wonderfully controversial. Jason promised to sign anything attesting to my calm and placid nature if he never had to listen again to me telling him how I had gotten into the habit of coming on little portraits of the Führer, imaging his moustache tickling my soft parts. How I found it hard to orgasm without doing the salute. I even offered to draw some of my dreams for him and suggested that role play might be a good way to overcome my tensions, but all he could mumble was that I should never forget that I am not my thoughts. Overall, I was quite disappointed with Jason and his lack of imagination, Dr. Seligman, yet there was one thing I was grateful for. Prior to those sessions I used to think of Hitler as nothing but a severe case of shortman syndrome gone horribly wrong. A desperate little moon trying to woo the sun when she couldn't care less. You might be wondering why I am referring to the sun as she, but remember that in my mother tongue the sun is a woman and the moon is a man, like some sort of Valkyrie trying to save her charms from an unpleasant little man. Maybe that is why we are so twisted and maybe that is why the so-called short-man syndrome has had such catastrophic consequences for us. I don't want to make amends again, but maybe Hitler really felt like he would not be able to satisfy the sun. Only a little man would come to think of his own potency in such terms; only he would feel threatened by someone that would never contemplate threatening him, who could not even produce his own light. I am sure that the sun does not care about the moon and his hopeless advances. Why would she even consider a man who could quite possibly walk into her vagina without any sentimental impact?

But even today, Dr. Seligman, for a German a living Jew is quite an excitement, something that no one prepared us for when we were growing up. We were only used to dead or miserable Jews, staring at us from endless grey photographs or from somewhere far away in exile, never smiling, and us forever in their debt. And our one way of making it up to you was by turning you into magical creatures with fairy dust coming out of every hole, with superior intellects, curious names, and infinitely more interesting biographies. In our imagination, no Jew would ever be a cabdriver, and there was even a page in my theology book dedicated to famous Jews. And in our music classes we had to sing "Hava Nagila" in Hebrew, Dr. Seligman—thirty German children and not a single Jew in sight, and we sang in Hebrew to make sure that we remained de-Nazified and full of respect. But we never mourned; if anything, we performed a new version of ourselves, hysterically nonracist in any direction and negating difference wherever possible. Suddenly there were just Germans. No Jews, no guest workers, no Others. And yet we never granted them the status of human beings again or let them interfere with our take of the story down to that ugly heap of stones they put up in Berlin to commemorate the victims of the Holocaust. Have you seen that, Dr. Seligman? I mean, seriously, who wants to be remembered like that? Who wants to be remembered as the receiving end of violence? We are so used to being in control of our victims, and that's why even after all these years I cannot quite suppress my amazement that you are alive outside our history books and memorial sites, that you have broken free from our version of you and that we're now in this room together doing what we are doing, that I can almost touch your lovely hair from up here. It's like a miracle. Although I should probably tell you that your hair is thinning a little at the crown; it's very slight, nothing that would deter an admirer. But still, I thought you should know.

Do you think it was silly of me not to make better use of Jason, Dr. Seligman? The one time they pay me to go and see a therapist, and I have nothing else to do but tell him such a mad story. I should probably be glad he did not have me committed and sent to some looney bin for coming up with nicknames for the Führer's cock. But that was the time before my body became the problem it is now, when I still thought I could just watch gay porn and somehow laugh my way out of this situation. That was before I met K, Dr. Seligman. Until then I had known about my dilemma, but there are different ways of knowing, of reacting to our knowledge. And contrary to what they say, you do need a body to love. All that rubbish about souls is simply not true, that you can love a soul independent of the shape it comes in. Our brains are made so that we can only love a cat as a cat and not as a bird or an elephant. If we want to love a cat, we want to see a cat, touch its fur, hear it purr, and get scratched if we get our petting wrong. We don't want to hear it bark, and if the cat started growing feathers, we would kill, study, and, finally, exhibit it as a monster. I don't know why our brains are like that, but K has taught me that if we try to grow feathers without people expecting us to fly, they will shoot us from the sky and their dogs will shake us to make sure our necks are broken before we are chucked into a bag and disposed of. Our brains can just about tolerate a cat with a missing tail or three legs, but any additions, anything the cat was not supposed to have been born with, will never be accepted. And a cat that barks is a sick cat that spent too much time in the company of dogs; it's not the kind of cat you want in your house for your children to play with, for who knows—its disease might spread, and the next day your Cockapoo will wake up with a horn in the wrong place. Until I met K, Dr. Seligman, I didn't realise that these are absolute borders that we are talking about, and that no barking cat has ever conquered the sky.

You know when you look back at your life and suddenly you can't pretend anymore that you didn't know something? In some ways, I have always known that I was a barking cat, and sitting here with you trying to understand my private parts, I have so many memories coming back. Did you have to go swimming with your mother as a child, Dr. Seligman? Did you have to share one of those small changing cubicles with one of your parents and wonder how long it would take for your own body to look exactly the same? When your pubic hair would start thinning and little warts would start growing under your armpits? I don't know why I couldn't just have waited outside, like all the other children. Maybe it was my mother's idea of intimacy, but I remember how her body used to terrify me, how I used to think it was the ugliest thing in the world, and every time her soft skin brushed against mine I felt like I was drowning in that little box of warmth and the smell of our old towels. Back then the word we used for public swimming pool was *badeanstalt*, swimming institution, but *anstalt* also is a short term for mental institution, and something about that terminology made those little cubicles feel even more uncomfortable, as though they were the first step toward a life spent in solitary confinement. To add to this, my mother had a scar from the caesarean that had helped me enter this world; it had not healed properly and looked like a shiny red worm, yet instead of being grateful I always despised her body even more for that stain, that overt mark of weakness. And I always wished she would hide all her tired skin in a bathing suit instead of holding on to her bikinis. Outside they would all be able to see that my body would look like hers one day, that my breasts would turn into those horrible saggy things, that purple stripes would show where my flesh had given in. They would see the whole tragedy of the female body paraded around in front of them at different stages of its development, like those stupid songs we had to sing in rounds at school. On and on and on. As soon as I was released from the four walls of shame, Dr. Seligman, I would search for the first male body I could find, to rest my eyes on a flat chest, feeding the secret hope that I might be spared, that my body would not change and that I would be allowed to carry on wearing my little swimming shorts. That one day my mother would stop threatening me with the horrors of her bodily existence.

You're right, it might be that my mother wasn't actually that ugly, but even later I could never get over the disappointment of the body, over the dis-

crepancies my illusions and all those useless mag-
azines for teenagers had produced. You see more
naked people than I do, Dr. Seligman, and I'm sure
you agree that all the excitement we have created
around the body isn't justified. It's just the illusion
that keeps us going, the fact that we have seen those
ancient statues and think that one day mortals like
that will be born again, that those are depictions of
actual human beings like you and me. I don't mean
to say that you are unattractive, Dr. Seligman—you
are of course a fine-looking man, even with your
hair loss and all—but, you know, nobody would
want one of us in marble. There is nothing about
us that would inspire music or poetry, that would
keep anyone awake at night, tortured with longing.
That's where we differ from animals: with very few
exceptions they always look the part, like perfect
representations of their species, dignified and in
just the right shape. That's why there are no ideal-
ised versions of tigers and panda bears, and only a
perverted mind would think of an ideal horse—you
know, those weird people that like to masturbate
next to a horse because everything else is illegal in
most countries. But looking out of your window
and seeing so many people that look like they are

about to go for a casting call for the *Hunchback of Notre Dame*, maybe they are right. What if they have seen the light and understood that you have to tell yourself so many lies before humans actually become attractive that you might just as well go and fuck a horse? And of course, horses don't talk, Dr. Seligman, it must be so much easier to love them.

I guess there is one moment when humans actually are beautiful. This is probably a sign that I have started to turn into a dirty old woman, but there is a moment of youth when their bodies are still firm and fresh, a bit like horses, when they have started to be adults without all the ugliness that comes with it. Before they are thinking about building houses and brushing their hair, before they are old enough to be mentioned in a will—that's the moment when you can still write poetry about them. Now I am past thirty and old; nothing was yesterday anymore, everything happened a few years ago. And my body's response to everything is haemorrhoids and horrible-smelling substances coming out of my orifices. I will never understand why my belly button sometimes goes soggy, Dr. Seligman, but I still remember that other age. Those years when all the creepy uncles come together and try to molest

you at family gatherings, when you are still confident that one day something interesting will happen in your life, before you realise that everyone
in your family is a boring cunt and, on the whole,
quite ill-disposed toward you. Before you realise
that your cousins are your worst competition and
that most lives are just endless repetitions of the
same mistakes, the same desperation, and the same
bad taste. I cut ties with most of my family years
ago, and even if that means that I will die alone
in a piss-ridden care home where carers will gag
me with their dirty underwear, it also means that I
managed to break free from the worst kind of conversation there is on this planet, that between family members, and in particular between aunts. It's
like sticking a hoover into your brain and pressing
reverse, except that there is no mercy: your head
won't simply explode, which would be a blessing.
Instead you will have to listen to that empty noise
for the rest of your life. Because blood is thicker
than water and you all climbed out of each other's
wombs one day. It's one of my few consolations,
Dr. Seligman—that I managed to leave that behind
and anyway, they would not understand what's
happening with me now. Most aunts don't even

understand if in life you don't just want to have children and die, so why would they understand this? And even if I tried to talk to them, all they would ask me is what happened to my great-grandfather's property after my grandfather's death. And I don't have an answer to that question, I mean, who knows what goes on in old people's heads? They are like children with money and even less of a moral compass; they are driven by the last desires they can afford, and in that quest, nothing will count as an inhibition. They scare me, Dr. Seligman, and sometimes I have nightmares about my grandfather's hands and the way they insisted on holding things they didn't have the strength for.

Are you sure you don't want to answer the phone, Dr. Seligman? I really don't mind. I quite like listening to your voice; unlike me, you have such a wonderfully British accent, too intelligent to be posh. And it might be an emergency, or maybe your wife. Is that her in the picture over there on your desk, or is that your mother, Dr. Seligman? With some men it's hard to tell who their heart belongs to, but I imagine that you are one of those happily married men with ironed pyjamas who could never imagine not being happy. And plus,

you are a member of a heavily persecuted minority,
so I am sure you have lots of children; they are your
form of rebellion. I get that, it must have been such a
triumph for you to get your wife pregnant and think
of all the people who tried to not make this possible. So, in a way, you are like me and think of Hitler
when you orgasm. I'm joking; I'm sure you thought
of flowers or how beautiful your wife was, and I'm
also sure that it was all very dignified. But don't you
think having someone's portrait on your desk like
that is a little possessive? Isn't adoring someone,
especially a woman, like burying them alive in your
own version of things? I always felt like men were
not capable of loving women for what they actually are, and so they turned them into little cakes,
or rather gâteaux—you know, those scary-looking
things we call torte in German. Something that's
nicely decorated and capable of keeping you alive
for many days if necessary, something that could
feed a family but not something you would ever buy
in a shop if it wasn't perfect. And at some point they
started calling this oppression love; I mean, I get it,
nobody likes ugly people, but I think it's a bit of a
stretch to label this a positive emotion as opposed
to something that we should all be working on, like

mindfulness and plastic straws. Just look at women in their wedding photos and then think of the horrible German torte with its layers and layers of buttercream, originally designed to help pensioners die more quickly, and all those men in suits smiling at yet another woman who fell for all this crap and let herself be turned into a pretty little thing, scared of moving in case some of her decoration will fall off, or that someone notices she wasn't born like this. That there is a face underneath this face and a heart beating underneath all those layers of white fabric, there to remind everyone of some seemingly long-forgotten tyranny of innocence and the generations of women that came before, who signed over their freedom for getting one day in their lives when they could honestly believe that they were the most fuckable thing in the room and that this was about them and not about conquering their spirits. Isn't loving someone like this a little like being with one of Mr. Shimada's sex machines, Dr. Seligman, or a dead person, someone who is defenceless and can no longer refute what is being said about them? I also wish it was more acceptable to speak ill of the dead; I feel like that way we could be closer to ourselves and our own history, and we wouldn't have to perpetuate the myth of how beautiful our grandmothers were and that they only grew their moustaches with old age instead of admitting that the fur on their faces could always rival a cat's whiskers. I wish we didn't feel this need to be proud of something that has no potential. But I'm sure you never tried to suffocate your wife in layers of buttercream, Dr. Seligman. You might even be a man with a romantic story who doesn't watch pornography, a man who would never contemplate the vices his money could afford.

Love often reminds me of blood, Dr. Seligman. Don't you think they are quite similar? Blood is only beautiful and full of symbols as long as it stays in its place, but once we see it smeared across someone's face or dried on a towel, we are put off, because our mind immediately fills in the gaps with violence and a lack of control. Love, like blood, needs to be a story we can tell. If it breaks free from the picture frames and veins we have forced it into, it causes hysteria, and brutal attempts are made to put it back where it belongs, to contain what is contagious; for, like love, blood gives life, but it is also home to all the things that can kill us, all that we are afraid of, all the diseases that Dracula instilled in his rats. There is a hygiene of love, don't you agree? Just like I cannot go smearing my blood around, like they have invented endless products to make sure women don't lose their dirty blood in public, I also cannot go around and just love where I see fit. The blood we see on the pavement could be anyone's; it's not immediately clear whether we are dealing with a person or an animal, and we don't even know how it got there, whether there is a culprit or whether they turned against themselves because they just couldn't handle it anymore. Whether they used a weapon or simply their teeth. Blood on the pavement signals unrest, just like love outside the frame, a reminder of all the pain that is inevitably coming our way. And don't get me wrong—I am not saying that I should be allowed to let loose in a playground, but we have such a clear idea of what a love story is that if you go and try to find a different way to use your heart, they will say that you too have sick rats in your basement and that you drank their blood when they least expected it. But it's their own fault, Dr. Seligman; if they had not tried to fit my body into one of their picture frames, to make me smile whilst nothing around me was true, I would never have tried to be like them, and K and

I would not have needed all those other colours to paint another universe onto each other's bodies.

K could cry like a child. He would sob and rub his eyes, and his bottom lip would protrude in defiance against the overall injustice of his fate. I don't know if he had taught his children to do the same, or if he had learned it from them, but afterwards he once told me that in those moments he actually felt like a child, like his body was little again, unable to escape the violence of others, the inevitable weakness of his own limbs, the force that forever outweighed his own efforts. The nausea you feel when your nose gets hit and you think you can smell your own blood. And so, he had found a way out of his body, and even if it was painful, he knew that our flesh holds many lies, that we should never trust the stories we find written on our skin. I think that's why we had to find each other. The first time he cried, Dr. Seligman, I just watched him as you would a wild animal that has suddenly chosen to show itself and not run away, and as with an animal, initially I didn't move, offered nothing as cheap as comfort, but simply watched as he returned to his former self. Shedding those big tears that rarely spring from an adult's eyes, those tears that still believe in adventures and shelter. Those tears that think that fairy tales are true, that sleep tight in the knowledge that the darkness outside their windows isn't real, that it's just a part of their parents' imagination. And afterwards his eyes were so clean. I have no better way of putting this, Dr. Seligman, but they were never red; instead they looked fresh. As if creation had only just happened, as if he had just unseen the world and the colours were suddenly all new to him. As if we could fall asleep every night knowing that our dreams would make us fly.

But I don't want to bore you with my broken heart and the whole story about K, Dr. Seligman. It seems like such a cliché to fall for an artist, and you must hear so many strange stories in your profession, all those bodies that need change, and who knows, you might not even approve of the fact that I have been with a married man. And also, Jason told me that I should try to be less focused on myself and that being interested in others might help me overcome some of my issues. But I find that really hard; most people are so dull, don't you think? I wish I could see the other frames on your desk from here—seven, I think? I am sure they contain pictures of your children and maybe even your grandchildren. I imagine that you got married when you were quite young and that your children followed your good example and always iron their clothes, and that you have regular family gatherings where you are all very loving and happy. Where even the occasional tragedy is part of the narrative. Would you forgive me if I was your child, Dr. Seligman? Your ugly German daughter, fallen out of your wife's precious womb like a rotten apple. I often think of my father when I do something wrong, and it always makes me so sad, because I know that he would never forgive any of it. And it's not that I have never contemplated pregnancy—it's the obvious thing to contemplate for someone my age, and I cannot turn on my computer without being bombarded with ads for pregnancy tests and nappies, images of all the happiness I am missing out on. And so I bought a "Baby on Board" badge to travel on the underground with; they were selling them in the market near work, and I thought, why not? We lie about so many things, why not about what goes on in our uterus? And already as I bought my little badge there was that smile, you know? The kind of smile you only get when someone thinks your life is complete and meaningful, when everyone can

37

see that you had sex for a reason and your body is finally no longer yours. I loved that smile, and for a while I became quite obsessed with wearing my badge and the power it suddenly seemed to grant me. I could ask people to bring me things for no other reason than because I was, as we would say in German, carrying another life under my heart. *Unterm herzen.* I don't pretend that I understood this sudden generosity, Dr. Seligman, when we all well knew that there was no reason to believe that this new life under my heart would turn out to be any less banal than that of everyone else. Yet still it's a holy moment, a moment as blue and beautiful as the Virgin Mary's gown, a moment when you finally become what you are. And I revelled in my holiness. I even made myself untouchable with dignity when I started to turn one of my rings around to make it look plain enough to be a wedding ring, plain enough to have a husband in a suit waiting for me at home. It was almost like finding a religion, like I was finally in a position to despise others.

Yet the badge also brought its limitations, and I stopped wearing it when I realised that it gave every last prick permission to stick a moral finger up my ass and drown me in a concern for the unborn, which they very rarely exhibited for anyone outside a womb. Even I know that nobody likes mothers. And even the concern for the unborn is a lie, Dr. Seligman. I mean, did you know that in all these years they never thought of inventing a seat belt for pregnant women, and that countless unborn children have been strangled by those unrelenting black things? I still remember them cutting into my neck when I was not sitting properly as a child and my mother telling me to straighten my back. It's the kind of unassuming material that will kill you in an instant, and it terrifies me, just like fishing rods and tights. There is no way they would break before you are strangled, and whilst there is maybe something sexy about playing with tights, it seems unacceptable to die from one of these other objects, to be strangled by one of life's many banalities. I cannot afford a car anyway, so I would be fine, but it still upsets me even now how everything, even time, is designed around the so-called male body, the body with a cock, putting half the population at risk of dying from objects of everyday use. And I am sure it applies to everything from toothbrushes to elevators, hot water bottles, pianos, and toilet seats. It could of course be that men are in need of all this extra assistance—you can't even have sex with them without their having an erection—but still I wonder, even though it doesn't really concern me anymore, don't you find it upsetting? Or is it not something you ever think about? I have often tried to understand the void at the other end of the outcry, why it is that men like you were happy to keep your better halves in a cage for so long? A cage measured to fit your own proportions, of course; it was always a tiger in a lion's cage with people saying there was hardly any difference between the two. And yet they all agreed that it would be unacceptable for the lion and his understanding of himself to be put in a tiger's cage. There's something inherently ridiculous about the tiger's cage, just like you might say that I would look quite dashing in your suit, Dr. Seligman, and people would think you had lost your marbles if you showed up in one of my old dresses or skirts. It would be the end of your masculinity—your life as a man—you would be a lion without a mane, weak and humiliated, and I never quite know whether this inspires my anger or my pity.

Have I told you that I like your small hands, Dr. Seligman? I know that a lot of women would not agree, but I think they are wonderfully soft and perfectly suited for your job. They almost feel like little kittens, warm right from the start; your wife must be so happy. And I don't see why everything about men always needs to be so oversized, why so many women feel the need to feel small. I think that's one of the reasons why, once my peachy years were over and the creepy uncles had moved on, men never took much interest in me; some parts of my body never seemed to belong to a woman, just look at my hands, I am sure they are bigger than yours, not to mention my feet, which have been a men's size ever since I hit puberty. Don't you think it's stupid to think about everything in that way when clearly it isn't true? For years, my feet alone made me feel like an ogre, not to speak of whole other industries of products designed for either men or women, of colours and smells associated with people with and without cocks. I could never understand why this had to be our primary way of looking at people, why we needed a system, down to public toilets, that separated the two. Personally, I have long started to use men's toilets, not just since I started dressing like one, partly because there are no queues, and partly to see what it feels like. In many ways it could be said that public toilets have taught me more about myself than most other places. Thinking of them as important spaces in our everyday lives, Dr. Seligman, it was there that I first felt excluded. It was there that I never shared secrets with my best friend, never reapplied my makeup, and never wrote the name of my sweetheart on a greasy wall. It was there that I felt for the first time that I didn't belong to a space made up exclusively of women and that I would never be able to share those moments of ecstasy, intimacy, and grief that seemed to bind them together in front of those tarnished mirrors. And it's not that I had no friends but the fact that I had to use these spaces because of the shape my body had turned out to be, just felt wrong, and so, once I had learned to think for myself, I started going to the men's toilets instead. And most importantly, Dr. Seligman, that's how I met K.

You want to know how I met someone in a public toilet? I wouldn't usually volunteer this information, but since you are asking, Dr. Seligman. Most men feel threatened when you come to check out their cocks in such a blunt manner, when you invade one of their last sanctuaries with open eyes, but not K. I could tell right from the start that he was

up for a challenge, and that all that happened afterwards was already defined in this moment. Please
don't think that I used to go to the men's toilets
looking for random sex, Dr. Seligman—that's not
what it was with K, it's just the way we met, nothing
more. And nothing less. I stood behind him, when
our eyes met in the mirror and I immediately forgot
that there was anyone else with us in that dismal
restroom at the back of a pub. Just like I forgot that
I had come there to pee; it was suddenly gone, my
whole body and all the obligations that came with it
were suddenly gone, and all that I could see was K's
cock. And he understood, and then—this gesture
still moves me, Dr. Seligman—he waited until all
the other men had left and washed himself in one of
those tiny sinks with separate taps for hot and cold.
That's when I knew that I could trust him, that it
was safe to disappear into one of those little cubicles with him. Maybe that is what I had been looking for in those toilets after all; maybe K was simply
the first to understand that all I wanted was to suck
off a complete stranger and leave it all behind.
The first who could read my silent gaze. I guess it
doesn't matter now, but it was the first time in my
life that I was ready to offer devotion, and I wanted

nothing else from him; I didn't want him to try and satisfy me. I just wanted to be there, squatting with my back against the wall and him holding my head firmly whilst he was fucking me in my mouth. I was content with his hands in my hair and my tongue licking the underside of his cock as he was gliding in and out. And when he offered to finger me afterwards, I declined, almost embarrassed that this was even a possibility. And yet I had never felt so satisfied before. You probably know more about this than I do, Dr. Seligman, but don't you think we are misled by our desire for orgasms?

I thought of my father whilst we did it. It's almost the reverse of watching your parents have sex, imagining how they could see you giving rough oral sex to a stranger in a dirty public toilet. I didn't do it because it turned me on, Dr. Seligman; I like the idea of others watching, but not like that, and I have not reached the point yet where I find satisfaction in letting my father down. I reached that point years ago with my mother, but with a mother it makes hardly any difference. It's not like you will ever be free from her love, from that animal-like affection that would follow its children to the darkest of dens, the kind of love that finds excuses for Marc

Dutroux and Harold Shipman. It's like the slime my mother covered me in before forcing me into this world, and the idea that I was once part of her flesh still fills me with dread. Her love was always too much, too embarrassing, too indiscreet. A father's love can't be compared to that; there is an element of choice in it—it's something you can win and, of course, something that you can lose. Gaining our father's love is, in many ways, our first achievement, have you ever observed how flirtatious babies are? They must know that nobody will respect them for their mother's love alone, and that everybody finds it so much more moving when we manage to conquer a reluctant heart. And just look at all the bad press single mothers get here in Britain and elsewhere; without your father's love, your chances of becoming a success are rather slim. We depend on it. I have no idea what it's like from the parental perspective and probably never will, but are you actually interested in your children beyond those seven frames, Dr. Seligman? Do you feel special for not walking out on them when they were little? Because we all know that you could have, and it would have been fine. Only women can't seem to get over the umbilical cord, have you noticed how when women leave their children to fulfil their dreams of money, younger men, and a happy vagina, they become monsters? How in our imagination they have all been seduced by the devil and have turned into immoral vessels of sodomy and lust? I sometimes think some women, once they realise what it means to be seen as a mother, they find a way to strangle their unborn children in the womb using the same umbilical cord that would otherwise have chained them to a life of self-annihilation and their mother-in-law's disgusting selection of homemade chutneys. And yet I never felt compassion. I never pitied my mother; if anything, I was angry that she had chosen to bring me into this world instead of doing away with me before anyone could notice. For not choosing to be free.

Did you talk very openly to your father, Dr. Seligman? I never told mine anything, because I always thought that silence was better than an open disappointment, than telling him a story he would never be able to understand. It's not like we spoke much anyway; my father was epileptic and mostly sedated from his medication and I don't think he had spoken much to his own father either. It wasn't something my father would have learned at home, where they all inherited my great-grandfather's silence. And so, I always feared that telling him what was really going on would bring about one of those terrible seizures. That he would die from choking on his own vomit just because I didn't understand how to be a girl. And yet it all started with him lying in bed on Sunday mornings, trying to recover from his life as a sales rep for washing machines. It's not a joke—that job really existed back then, and once a year he even got to go to the annual conference on the development of washing machines that took place in Nuremberg. The sinister irony of that only became apparent to me much later, Dr. Seligman, but really, which other city would be desperate enough to host such an event? Where else would they have wet dreams about clean laundry, endless washing lines with freshly laundered shirts floating in the summer air —we even had a TV advert propagating that stupid image. Anything to make people forget about the other annual event that used to take place there and the famous laws named after the city separating people into human and subhuman categories, deciding by means of the most dilettantish little pie charts who deserved to live and who didn't, who had fucked the wrong way and who hadn't. And the best thing they could think of, apart from the annual conference on the development of washing machines, was to put on that ghastly Christmas market, which is nothing but a facade to cover up their lack of grief. It's their way of pretending that this is all that ever happened there, that since medieval times they have always just been selling overpriced wooden crap and that all they ever used their ovens for was to make *lebkuchen*—you know, that famous German ginger-bread. It's so typical, this inability to acknowledge that they have lost far more than their architecture makes me so angry, Dr. Seligman, and to think that now they are also hosting these Christmas markets here in London makes me feel sick to the core. Why won't they just leave people alone?

Anyway, my mother often sent me to wake my father as he lay in bed on Sunday mornings, and I knew that underneath the blanket I would pull away, he was usually naked. People often think that the German approach to nudity is very avant-garde, that it's a sign of our liberation, but thinking of my father's nudity now, it doesn't strike me as a symbol of freedom, Dr. Seligman; if anything, I think it's a way of showing that you have nothing to hide. That

your body is healthy and that you have not grown
a third nipple or a lazy foot, that you have not acci-
dentally fucked a Jew and polluted the entire race.
That you are scared of mysteries. There was nothing particularly inspiring about this nudity, and yet,
looking at his penis in the silence of my parents'
bedroom, I had a very strange thought. And it's
not like I could see much—it was mostly hair and
testicles, a perfect example of modesty—and still I
suddenly thought that maybe it was possible to buy
one in a shop. That somewhere between Barbie
dolls and Play-Doh containers would be a section
where I could find my own cock; that's how simple
I thought it was. I didn't think there was more to
it, I just liked the idea of getting rid of my *scham-
lippen*. You probably know this, Dr. Seligman, how
in German labia are called lips of shame; and even
today I cannot pronounce the word without feeling
embarrassed, and I would never have summoned
the courage to look for a pair of those in a shop.
But I did check the blue and pink aisles at the local
toy shop for a cock whenever I got the chance, and
of course I searched in vain. Not even male teddy
bears or robots were allowed genitalia, and there is
not much to be said about the funny little mound

between Ken's legs. I doubt that even the shop assistant was allowed to bring his own cock to work, and so there was nothing for me there. I later forgot about this thought and didn't rebel when they put me into dresses and forced me to grow out my horrible curly hair, and I only once managed to cut off my eyelashes. It never occurred to me that this was my first attempt to express my true feelings, that there was more to it than childhood weirdness. I hear that things are changing now, Dr. Seligman, and that even small children are encouraged to go shopping for the genitalia of their choice, but back then a girl was a happy shape growing around a vagina with everyone hoping that it would turn out fresh and tight. The rest didn't matter.

I also wouldn't have known quite what to say about K. I usually find it hard to describe people, and we didn't talk much about those things that are meant to define us, like jobs and haircuts. And anyway, I had been fired for threatening my colleague with a stapler, and K was a painter whose wife paid the bills. There wasn't that much to say, really, and I never actually told him how I lost my job. I never even worked out where K was actually from. He spoke with one of those accents that are foreign, but don't give a clue about where this foreignness might come from, and unlike me, he didn't suffer from a compulsion to talk about his *heimat*. It was actually quite the opposite with him, and I understood quite quickly that he didn't like to talk about his origins, or roots, or however you want to call it. And anyway, it has become such a useless question to ask—where are you from? I think that people should be allowed to decide for themselves, and they might feel different at different times; they might wake up every morning and decide that they are from a different place. It's not for us to decide. But that's not what K did. I think he just removed that question from his mind, and when we were together, Dr. Seligman, it was as if all the maps had been taken off the wall and we could stop being all the things you have to be as a functioning human being. Suddenly, there were no continents, no surnames, no parents, no jobs, no children, and, as far as it was possible, no bodies. Without agreeing to do so, we made it a thing not to call anything by its name, not to talk of cocks and vaginas and not to make love the way we had both been taught. Making love is such a stupid phrase anyway; how can you make an emotional state? And why is it never referred to as making hate or boredom or despair? And yet sometimes, especially after K had allowed me to play with some of the colours in his studio and to paint on his body, when he watched me move those red and pink shades across his skin, he sometimes looked so relieved, Dr. Seligman, as if something had been restored to him that he had lost a long time ago. And I always longed for the moment when he would just take a little too much purple and smear it across my face, very slowly, and never any other colour. And then he would start laughing, for it's not only that he could cry like a child, he could also laugh like one. And there was something so irresistible about the freedom he took in the face of the world. It was like he couldn't remember the last time something had actually mattered to him, like he would paint over anything that stood in his way and bury it under his very own shade of purple. Like I too could disappear under those acrylic floods.

That's also what worries me about Mr. Shimada's sex machines, Dr. Seligman. Someone will have programmed them before they are sent off, and even though they are not real, artificial intelligence, not the kind of machines we see in films, I still believe that most sex requires some form of consciousness, don't you think? Surely most people would give their robot a name, and that's why I am worried that it will have been programmed to love me despite the fact that I will be the one taking advantage. Do you know what I mean? The idea just makes me feel uncomfortable; raised as a woman, I have not been taught how to accept sexual favours, and so I have been wondering whether my robot could have different settings, maybe my robot could be allowed to express his aversion toward me and my strange sexual needs. Eventually we could fall out, and like a cat he could trade me in for a different owner, which, of course, I would do nothing to prevent, just like I let people skip queues or make jokes about me when I try to order something in a café. Someone even once told me that I had a childish face, as if they had seen me make my drink bubble by blowing into a straw. Some days it feels like I am wearing a big red nose that only I can't see, and that not even my sex robot—let's call him Martin, Dr. Seligman—that not even Martin, who is really just a talking dildo, would take me seriously. That nothing will ever make your reality go away. That there will always be days when all your scars awaken and you can still hear all the words and laughter that seemed to follow you around. When you can feel all those old aches and bruises, the crushed tissue and blood that's no longer yours. When life seems like nothing but a collection of moments when you lost control, nothing but a row of blind spots in your dignity, and all you can do about it is to fuck a heap of nonrecyclable material with an artificial voice. I guess it would be better for the planet if we stuck to humans—to bear in mind the ecological balance of our actions.

You probably think that I'm a coward, Dr. Seligman, for not using the proper word to describe Martin, because it's one of those words that has the potential to be so offensive that everyone will think your grandmother had a fling with the devil and soon you will start growing a clubfoot and a spiky cock the size of a house. I am scared of those words; I know what language is capable of, that language never lies, but since we are alone and your velvety walls will shield us from anyone's hearing range, I might as well own up to the fact that buying Martin would be a form of exploitation, of sexual slavery. Because it all begins with that mind-set, and I cannot prove that it is not in our nature to subject others to our power and our will, to break their bodies and their souls, and that we are constantly trying to paint a picture of human nature that doesn't exist. That there are no friendly urges. And even though Martin will have been programmed to smile when I enter him, this smile will have no actual foundation in a real situation; it will not be based on any human behaviour. And I am worried that it will pervert my mind, Dr. Seligman, that, given my heritage, it will trigger the monster inside me and gradually I will start thinking that Martin is real and that I can treat real people like him. That I will forget what a human being is and try to fuck people against their will, or worse. But then, with this new slavery and all those new devices and gadgets that are constantly at our disposal like delirious lapdogs, there's an irony that previous forms of slavery were lacking. Unlike with the more traditional forms of slavery, where people are reduced to their bodies with the overall aim of making them extinct in the process or torturing them to death and destroying all proof that they ever existed, the kind of slavery that made us all so rich, these new electronic slaves are burying us alive. Have you noticed, Dr. Seligman—or maybe you are lucky enough to be too old for this kind of modernity—how all these new slaves are designed to keep us in the house? How they deprive us of all human contact by bringing us our food and our shopping and our orgasms whilst drowning what's left of our brains in endless TV programmes? How they will fuck and feed us until we forget how to spell our own name? Until we forget that we are not the picture we see of ourselves on a screen? Until what's left of our useless bit of personality is isolated by comfort and silence.

And when we are actually forced to talk about ourselves, things always get so awkward, because there's really very little to talk about. Do you also sometimes have to go to some form of work drinks, Dr. Seligman? The kind of thing where it's not clear whether people smell of piss or coffee, where they make conversation until everybody is so bored that they are ready to roll down a hill in a barrel full of nails? When I still had a job, my only way out of these situations has always been to lie and pretend I came from Berlin and to then stop listening when people would start rattling off their relentlessly predictable anecdotes. It's what being German in London is mostly about—pretending that you are from Berlin and that you have read Max fucking Sebald. It works every time. But then I don't really understand the purpose of all this modern way of travelling, Dr. Seligman. Don't you agree that it's a tragic delusion to think that anyone has ever learned anything from their three months in Amsterdam or Hanoi? If anything, it usually makes them even more of a twat, because people always think that they have suddenly acquired a fashionable form of otherness that entitles them to the assumption that something worth mentioning happened in their lives. That, as if by some magic trick, they have become different, but different in a good way. I have much more respect for people who go on the same, banal holiday on some Mediterranean beach every year instead of turning their vacation into a statement. I'm sure you make very sensible holiday choices, and I can picture you exchanging your glasses for one of those timeless pairs of shades, Dr. Seligman, taking your wife to dinner like you used to all those years ago. You are not like those people who suddenly grow a beard and travel the globe riding a stuffed cat, going to local bars and eating street food and then come back and explain these other cultures to you. These people just upset me, Dr. Seligman; they are like American films about the Holocaust, they turn everything into a cliché until you feel like you're being fucked by Ronald McDonald and you wish there was an electric fence somewhere nearby. I don't even know when everything became so ridiculous that I often struggle to leave the house, because I see no way back to how we could become real people again. You are probably right in thinking that this is something I could have spoken to Jason about, that this could be seen as part of my anger, but I didn't threaten my colleague because of his holiday in Mexico, and I even accepted the little souvenir of a glittery, multicoloured skull with grace. I even smiled when he told me about those white beaches and all the mezcal he drank and I didn't point out that in order to get to all those places he had probably passed several mass graves of violently disappeared people, mostly women. I am not that kind of person, and that was even before Jason told me that I have to learn to be happy for others and that by not judging others I could be more generous toward myself, that I could train my mind not to react to those triggers anymore. But I felt that if I did that, there wouldn't be much left of me, that I would become mellow and gradually disappear, and so I just continued to lie to him.

I understand why you're asking that, Dr. Seligman, but I'm not always like that, and it is quite possible, that if Jason had been able to appreciate the aesthetic significance of velvet, I wouldn't have been quite so mean. It was really your love of velvet that convinced me when we first met that you were the right choice, and it goes so well with that aftershave of yours. There is something about this dark red velvet on your walls and chairs that made me think you were a serious person, someone I could respect and trust with this task. I think that a lot of other plastic surgeons have become vulgar with the money they make and the people they treat, but not you, Dr. Seligman; there is not even a hint of glamour about you. And for some reason I cannot lie looking at velvet, maybe because it speaks of power whilst at the same time it's so delicate, it's one of those eternal combinations we seek to seduce ourselves with. Jason, on the other hand, was based in one of those contemporary rooms where it's impossible to tell whether you are sitting in a café, an office, a shop, or someone's living room, and I am still not quite sure what it was. All that avocado aesthetic made my senses go numb, and as soon as I set foot in that room, I felt compelled to lie to him. It wasn't a space for honesty. But because even I struggled to fill all those sessions with enough material about the Führer's cock and how we would occasionally involve his dogs in our little games, I told him about how I sometimes follow strangers. I don't remember how I came up with the idea, but I guess something fascinated me about how much power you can gain by overstepping those small boundaries. Most people would be terrified if you suddenly stared in through their windows, and that's not even illegal—just like following them is mostly within the law. I think that most perversions are born out of a sense of insignificance, Dr. Seligman, and telling Jason all about them was like a fun way to try them out, another way of leaving myself behind. And it's quite easy to follow someone; have you ever tried it? There are so many different lives in this city, you can't look into any direction without facing someone else's reality, and sometimes it scares me to think how many other people around me are breathing, sleeping, taking showers, and using up resources right now, how many other ways of doing things there are. I grew up in a small town, so often I can't quite believe that there are so many of us here. And yet there will be so few people whose lives you will ever get to know, and now that I have chosen to come and see you, I am more scared of loneliness than I ever was before. You have filled those seven frames on your desk with loving faces, you have built your fortress against loneliness, or at least you think you have, but I won't be able to do that anymore, and it frightens me. What if, like Frankenstein's monster, I end up perving on other people's domestic bliss just to be chased away like a dirty pigeon, my limbs rotten from my own disgrace. I'm exaggerating, I know; the family was as unhappy as the monster, and he was lucky to get away and ruin their lives from a distance. K always told me that we don't have the ability to make each other happy and that we should just accept loneliness as part of the human condition. That there is no way out of our skin and that we are all born with a broken heart. He thought that's what they meant by original sin.

I never told Jason about my fear of loneliness, Dr. Seligman; I didn't want to offer him any inroads for his positivity crap, and so I just told him about Helen, the woman from my commute. I am not usually interested in women; their bodies tend to remind me of my own obligations and fill me with dread. I can never sit next to pregnant women without feeling a mild panic creeping up my throat and my chest suddenly getting very tight. But there was something about Helen that interested me. I gave her that name because I thought it was suitable. She had a little beauty mark and she reminded me of Bambi, her eyes slightly too big for her head and always filled with the kind of fear that men like to protect women from. It's one of the many embarrassments of my life that I only recently realised that Bambi was supposed to be a boy and that the film is based on a pornographic Austrian novel, which I rather like. Bambi the horny stag. Now I would have to name Helen after something else—definitely not a deer, but back then it seemed suitable. She was petite, her hair was blond and carefully blow-dried to make it look wavy, she was dressed according to the latest fashion, and she was wearing an engagement ring on one of her slender fingers. I liked the way she touched her lips as she was eating her morning croissant, pretending that she was one of those women who wouldn't gain weight, and I was wondering how she could bear to be like everyone else. She must have known that armies of other women in London wore the same ring, used the same chemicals to dye their hair, came home to the same stupid men, and dreamt of that wedding in Tuscany. But Helen seemed content, even though her fiancé had most likely proposed to her at a public monument, on a beach, or at their favourite restaurant, run by spiteful foreigners that they patronised by finding their choice of terrible decorations original, and I accused myself of bitterness and jealousy. Why couldn't I accept that some women derive happiness from their vaginas and their femininity? Why did I always have to think of it as a weakness? And so, I followed my Catholic roots and tried to repent. Prior to that I had only associated being on my knees with a comfortable position for masturbation, but suddenly I wanted to learn to accept what life had in store for me and that I too could be like Helen. I think up to that point Jason was quite happy with my story, with my unexpected desire to become neat and manageable, to get rid of my pubic hair and start resembling a peach. And even when I told him how I imagined Helen's sex life—especially her husband's body, his firm cheeks and solid cock—he still seemed relieved that we had moved on from Nazi sex and how hearing Adolf's voice still gave me uncontrollable erections, years after our imaginary breakup. I had suddenly returned to being an underfucked cat lady who objectified men, which must have seemed like the more acceptable crime. He looked decidedly more uncomfortable when I told him that I had started following Helen, because seeing her in the morning simply wasn't enough. And when I revealed that I was planning to break into her house—one of those houses with a purple magnolia tree in the front garden—whilst she was holidaying on a Greek island, I saw the first signs of genuine despair on his face. I told him that I meant no harm, but it's just that once I get to know someone, I always want to masturbate in their bath and steal a little souvenir, an object of their everyday, like a teabag, a pen, or, in some instances, some of the hair I find on their pillows. Are you laughing, Dr. Seligman? Jason surely wasn't, and I could tell that he thought I had locked Helen up in my basement. It's possible that he also thought I was Austrian; Germans don't usually bother with basements—they are happy to torture people on the first floor, they're not that discreet. They don't have the reputation of one of those old-fashioned empires to live up to. And Jason also didn't understand that there is nothing like masturbating in places that mean something to you, and how you will never forget them in your entire life. It's like they all become your home, and that, apart from killing ourselves, it's the only true freedom we possess. To give ourselves pleasure when we feel like it. I am sure you agree, Dr. Seligman; I mean, why else would you have velvet on your walls?

Of course I am okay with your taking pictures. Your assistant told me that this would be part of the examination today, but thank you for checking—and don't worry, I will hold still. I can't help but think that Jason was ungrateful, though; he didn't even appreciate that I tried to acknowledge my situation, whatever that might mean, but I thought he would be pleased that I was aware that I even had a situation. I also didn't want him to grow suspicious, because I couldn't afford to be sued by my ex-colleague; my inheritance won't stretch to that, and it's only a matter of time before my aunts start making demands. And I guess a small part of me also wanted to feel sorry for Jason. With people like him, it's a little bit like in one of those Western films: you have to shoot first, because if you don't feel sorry for them, they will feel sorry for you, and it's only downhill from there. And I like to make people feel incompetent, because I never felt like I was good at anything, so why should anyone else? I am sure you have never been in a situation like this, Dr. Seligman; you would never allow a character like Jason to make you question your beliefs. You are too sure of yourself and your ways, you know how to live your life, and you don't need any help with it. Unlike most men, you know the difference between a woman and a bicycle. That's a very attractive quality, Dr. Seligman, and useless people like myself get very attached to the kind of guidance you offer, we are like the seagulls that follow ships across the ocean, intoxicated by this sudden sense of direction and purpose. But people like Jason only live off making others feel bad about themselves, by pretending that they know the way when in the end they will drown just like everyone else, and for no apparent reason. Like the boy in that stupid *Titanic* film. We all know that there would have been enough space for him on that plank, but we also know that this was the only way to turn this into a love story. To pretend that she would have married him, to relish a broken heart rather than reality. Nobody wants to marry their holiday fling, and women cannot save men from poverty, unless they are old pervs; only Jasmine was allowed to save Aladdin, but then she also had a tiger for a pet. You can't really mess with that.

Please don't think that I am a sociopath, Dr. Seligman. I know that we need illusions, but sometimes I think that we shouldn't be so scared of the truth. And I don't mean the truth about how most olive oil is fake or one in three beards contains traces of faeces—those facts aren't fun, and it's probably best to keep lying to ourselves about them and the damage we do to ourselves and others. But what about beauty? Don't you think we would all be happier if we could finally get over that illusion? When I was younger, my best friend had been to see a fortune-teller and kept scaring me with stories about an impending war, World War III. Do you know what my first stupid thought was? That I could finally eat as much chocolate as I wanted, that suddenly it didn't matter anymore if I was fat or not, that some higher power had finally taken control of my body. And remembering the skinny pictures of my grandmother from after the war, Dr. Seligman, I was so excited that I would soon be free from all those petty concerns for my protruding belly and my mother's fear that my bum might get too big and that it would start wobbling. It was thanks to her that I always knew that a body could be ugly and that whatever you do in life, you don't want any of your body parts to wobble. And until this day I have not been able to free myself from her perspective. I can forever see the light of changing rooms shining on my ugly curves, revealing everything I wish she hadn't seen. But back then I decided that I would go and buy white chocolate, as many bars as my measly pocket money would allow, and that I would hide them from my mother and eat them when I was alone, safe in the knowledge that my body had more or less ceased to exist in the face of this catastrophe. It was only much later and after I had eaten all the chocolate and no bombs had fallen outside my window that I realised that no catastrophe, apart from maybe a final nuclear strike, would ever be big enough to free us from this curse. That even though we're in charge of this planet, we are its ugliest inhabitants, and that our longing for our own beauty will never cease, that we will never be content with the beauty in front of us. And yet I will never forget the feeling with which I ate that chocolate, Dr. Seligman; nowadays it gives me a headache if I eat more than just a little bit, but in that moment it was a sin without consequences. And I never gave up on the dream that one day my body wouldn't matter anymore. It's a little bit like imagining that your glasses are sunglasses, Dr. Seligman; the light gets easier to bear.

Together with the same friend, I also used to watch a lot of music videos. I never cared much for the music, and I never felt like they were singing for people like me. But there was something about that condensed extravagance that fascinated me— those perfect bodies and how they could deal with anything in the course of three minutes. How you could remain attractive in the midst of any calamity. Nothing seemed to matter as long as you could dance, and someone did your makeup, you could fit any story into those few lines, and I started to watch the charts every Saturday morning in my friend's bedroom. My parents would never have paid for those other channels, for the fun programmes and all that American stuff, for the commercials. And they wouldn't have understood why I drew comfort from this parallel universe, from these people who had just left their ordinary existences behind and now lived off glitter and fame, who liked the idea of complete strangers having posters of them in their bedrooms. I admired their confidence, and because of those videos I even thought that there was a certain elegance to them and that their movements were real. You are probably laughing again down there, but I wasn't fooled by their lyrics, and back then nobody sang about what it's like when a boy is stuck in a girl's body and wants to fuck boys. I am not even sure anyone does today, as pop culture is not actually that subversive and needs to be sellable in places where people aren't free. But I was misled by their bodies, and you have to become pretty old before you see that if you ever tried to walk down the street in one of those outfits, even if you had one of those perfect bodies, you would be a rather tragic sight and that we were all raised on so many sweet images that I am surprised we can all bear to look at each other. Yet after a while, as I was sitting there with my best friend, I could always detect a little red glow on her face—these images turned her on. But no matter how hard I tried, they did nothing for me; my vagina remained dumb and numb as if it had been made with Play-Doh from the toy shop, disfigured and useless. And it's not that I hated them because I was one of those people who hate things because little girls like them, it just took me so long to understand my own desires, Dr.

Seligman, to understand that I was forever one step removed from fulfilling them and that choosing my favourite boy band member, which I then struggled to remember, would always be a lie because my body was the wrong recipient. Because my body didn't exist. Because I couldn't see these boys with a girl's eyes. I think that's why I developed an early liking for the opera and the theatre; that was also weird, but a kind of weirdness that people had heard about and were more willing to accept. And I felt more at ease in a world of costumes and allegories where at least occasionally you would see a woman dressed as a man or men dancing in tights, moving in ways I had never seen before. Bodies that were not designed to speak to boys and girls but that spoke to a different set of senses, that went deeper than anything I had experienced before, and I fell madly in love with this world where, for a few hours, anything was possible and you could be highly emotional for no reason. Back then I longed to live on a stage, Dr. Seligman, to be allowed to go around in a costume of my own choosing.

This love of the stage was one of the things I shared with K. He too seemed mesmerised every time the curtain went up, and I could feel a childlike excitement electrifying him. He told me that to him it had always been a safe space, a space where you knew in advance what horrors to expect. It was also one of the few spaces where we could sit in the dark amongst other people and pretend to be like them, one of hundreds of other Thursday-night couples holding hands to show their affection. They had no idea what was going on beneath my skirt, and I could tell that he was becoming more and more reckless; he knew full well that we might run into one of his many acquaintances—as a married man, K knew many friends of friends—but he didn't care. He just told me that his wife didn't like the theatre and that it was very important for him to come here with me, that it helped him to cope with things. And it took me a long time, Dr. Seligman, to work out what his demons were. It wasn't his body, because unlike me, he had a pop star's confidence in his appearance and his movements, and so I spent many hours next to him in the dark, wondering what it was that made him run away from his perfect life to come and be with me and my increasingly dysfunctional vagina. But then it's one of my many flaws, Dr. Seligman, that I cannot imagine other people's unhappiness. I felt so violated by society all my life that I refused those people who lived by its rules the right to be unhappy. I always wanted them to smile themselves to death for supporting those institutions and limitations that had made everything so difficult for me, for thinking that as long as you tick all the boxes and follow all the rules, flowers will be growing out of your ass until the end of time. I didn't want them to be allowed to talk about their pain; I wanted them to suffer from their own stupidity, to starve like that Greek king in the midst of all their fucking happiness. And even with K. I saw a picture of his wife once, she was pretty—you know, a bit like Helen, one of those women who don't mind being a woman, and it took me the longest time to accept that he was lonely in the midst of all his happiness and that he too felt the pressure of having to smile in family pictures, or to smile in general. You know how nowadays we are constantly expected to have a good time? How people put on their broadest smiles for health insurance ads and verruca treatments? If it was up to them, we would all continue to smile in our sleep, and the worst thing is that these people perceive it as a criticism when you don't smile back at them or refuse to have fun. If you were a regular plastic surgeon, Dr. Seligman, I would ask you to silence those muscles in my face, to put an end to this industry of happiness.

Are you scared of dogs, Dr. Seligman? Or, rather, of those men who mostly live what remains of their sexuality through their pets' oversized genitalia? Apparently, men first look at a dog's private parts before they see anything else—like victims of their own dreams. Just think of all the dog ladies they have been perving on and all the male ones they tortured because they felt inferior. And yet these men often refuse to have their dogs neutered; they are worried that it will reflect badly on their own unused cocks. But then I never worried about these dogs, never felt like they would turn their doting little faces against me. Until K told me about his fear of dogs, it simply never occurred to me that some of them were like unlicensed weapons on a leash, that those teeth could rip my flesh apart, that those jaws were strong enough to chew my bones. At first it was so strange for me, Dr. Seligman, because if you saw K, you would think that he was a big man, gifted with the kind of physique that is meant to remain unharmed. But the body others see is never the body we see, and whenever he saw a dog, he would cross the street; just walking next to him, I could feel his body freeze with fear. I found it very upsetting that his pride was so vulnerable, that everyone could see that there was a wound his skin had never been able to cover. It was like watching someone being hit with their own hand. We never discussed this fear, just like we didn't discuss his fear of the dark, because I always think that there is nothing more private than fear, and K was a real collector of fears. It would have taken more than a lifetime to archive them all. What do you think of when you hear the word fear, Dr. Seligman? I think of a part of my body that I don't know, but I am sure exists, pink flesh from before I was born. Something that doesn't want to be touched because it has no skin yet to protect itself, like a version of me that never got the chance to live and is breathing somewhere in the dark, scared of being discovered by the wrong hands. Moist and unshaped. But you, Dr. Seligman—do you think of angst? Of my ancestors in their uniforms and their dogs? K made me think a lot about that image, about how much it adds to violence if you outsource it to an animal that was born without intentions, that would have protected you under different circumstances. An animal that had its dignity taken away in order for you to be relegated to its rank. And yet they wouldn't even have given you the chance to be a gladiator; they went straight for the humiliation, for the power of those who think they have corrupted nature to their advantage—which brings me to another concern of mine, Dr. Seligman. Violence is such a male toy, and I feel that by going through this process I am opening myself up to those possibilities. I am taking the risk of becoming one of those sausage-faced German men in need of a large canine penis, and it worries me, Dr. Seligman, it really does.

I guess it is one of the reasons why I came to see you; to be honest, it's probably the main reason, and I know this might sound a little strange, Dr. Seligman, but when I was younger I always thought that the only way to truly overcome the Holocaust would be to love a Jew. And not just any old Jew, but a proper one, with curls and a skullcap. Someone who's devout and can read from the Torah and doesn't leave the house without a black hat. I know that this was in poor taste, and I am only telling you this to make you understand where I am coming from, and maybe also to confess that I've always had a thing for those curls. I myself went through a phase of pretending that I still had that wavy hair I used to hate so much by rolling up my curlers every night, and I loved the idea of a man doing the same; it suddenly made everything more fluid, and I felt less like a girl for doing so. I kept thinking what it would be like to unroll each other's curls in the morning, how gentle it would be. But of course it's nonsense to think that you can overcome a crime on someone else's behalf and that my otherwise useless vagina could suddenly become a symbol of peace by welcoming one of those beautiful circumcised cocks. And where we lived there were no Jews anyway, not even a reminder that they had once lived there—nothing but that strange German silence that I have come to dread more than anything else. That way of pretending that everything has been swallowed by the ruins. I would have had to leave for one of the bigger cities to find my Jew, and whilst I liked the idea of telling my father and maybe even my grandfather about my plans, I didn't have the courage to go in search of my Shlomo. That's how I referred to my new romance, Dr. Seligman. I had always liked that name. I am not even sure my father would have shown much of a reaction—his medication would have hidden much of his despair—and yet I would have liked to explore those soft parts of my family, that tissue which has grown around our past. To try and reach across that gap that stands between ourselves and what we could have been if we hadn't decided to change things forever in a moment of genocidal rage. I was never really able to fully grasp what we have done, Dr. Seligman, what it means to wipe out an entire civilisation, but I always felt that I had grown up in a ghostly country in which there were more dead than living, where we lived in cities that had been built around the remnants of where our cities used to be, and every day felt like walking on something that wasn't supposed to be there. I always felt like we had wiped out ourselves too. And I always thought that by finding Shlomo I could find a way back to how things used to be, to retrieve a fragment of what has been so irretrievably lost. But of course there is no way back, and I very much doubt that I could have tempted poor Shlomo with my private parts and I really admire your courage, Dr. Seligman, for laying your hands on a German vagina. And I want to promise you that it will all be worth your while, for not only are you making sure that I will never give birth, but you are giving a German woman a Jewish cock. That's much more radical than my affair with Shlomo could ever have been, don't you think? It's like the *übermensch* is finally becoming real. I can almost feel the sun rising above my head and the trumpets getting ready in the background as we walk down hand in hand, confident that this is the true victory. That this time it will be a peace project. We should probably have considered applying for EU funding; our project could have been called something like "Exchanging Shapes and Minds: How Having a Jewish Penis Changed My Life." Don't you think, Dr. Seligman? We could have been famous.

I know you asked me this earlier, but I haven't told anyone yet that I have come to see you. It's not that I'm ashamed but I prefer to tell people about things after they have happened. I like the inevitable. I will of course have to tell my parents, eventually, but, you know, my mother always wanted me to become a teacher—a lady teacher—and not someone who got fired from a third-rate admin job and spent a small fortune on a cock. So, this will be hard for her, and she will also wonder where I got the money from. And the wish to become a teacher was passed down from my grandmother, who could never become a teacher because, as with my mother, there was not enough money to let a woman study, and when my mother met my father and the washing machines, it was already too late. But then, life always gives you the option to trouble your children to make up for your own failures. Even if you haven't achieved anything, you can always fuck someone and let your children get on with it, though my parents do of course have a romantic wedding picture to prove the sincerity of their emotions. I was not just the product of their own disappointment, or so they say. But I let them down anyway, and nothing makes me see the absurdity of my situation more clearly than when I try to imagine myself as one of those German lady teachers, proudly owning her breasts in front of a room full of teenagers who would have had to call me Frau Göring-Mengele, or Bormann-Speer, or simply Fräulein Adolf. Just imagining it makes me laugh—me in charge of educating the young, living a life that's immediately understandable for everyone. It's not that I don't sometimes envy those people, Dr. Seligman; when I feel low I do wonder how much my little bit of freedom is really worth and whether there was no way I could have pulled myself together, made peace with my breasts, and made generations of children hate music and literature. I never had a brain for science. But there was no way I would have lasted, for if you decide to live such a life, you really have to live it, and if people get wind of the fact that you like to suck off strangers in public toilets, they will not trust you with their children anymore. And they will come after you with their pitchforks once they realise that it was their husband you had between your lips. As a woman I would have had to get married to not be a source of danger, and that was always out of the question for me. I have never dreamt that dream, Dr. Seligman, not even as a girl.

And still I believe that K would have found me anyway, and he wouldn't have cared about a ring on my finger, and I wouldn't have cared either. Nothing would have stopped us from playing our games, and he would have made me go back to those places regardless. It's not that we could not afford the occasional hotel room, but it turned K on to play games in public. With everything K did, Dr. Seligman, he was always looking for exposure in safe spaces, and I have never met anyone less private than that man. His favourite game was to make me go with a man of his choosing and to listen at the door. You might be appalled by this, Dr. Seligman, but I trusted K from the first minute, and I loved being dominated in that way; and I also loved the thrill of never knowing whether we had just met up for a drink or whether he had other plans for me. And when I had been naughty, he would pick a particularly unattractive man for me, one of those who can only ever hope for a pity fuck. It's surprisingly easy to offer oral sex to strangers; it's almost like it doesn't count because there is never the risk of making a baby, because it's not really an encounter of two equal bodies but more the mouth as a source of relief. But I never minded any of that; I had become indifferent to this body and what happened to it, because I think by that point I had already taken my decision to come and see you, and my time with K was almost like the kind of party you celebrate in a house that you know will be demolished. It's all without consequences. And I did enjoy those other games too, when he made me lie down on the floor of his studio and told me to masturbate whilst he was working, walking around, or taking phone calls, and I wasn't allowed to stop until he told me to. I had never experienced such pleasure before, and yet it bothered me that for some of those games I always had to play the part of a woman. I understood that K could only pick straight men for our games, but I think it angered him when he saw me looking at those other men, those who made love to each other, because he wasn't possessive when it came to things that he too could offer; he knew that he was good at it. But those other things—he didn't like it when he could see me longing for them, Dr. Seligman, and when I realised that K was more than I thought he was, it was too late. When I realised that I had become precious to him, and that it's not true that the reddest stars are always the coldest.

I don't want to be mean again, and I know that in some strange way he could even be considered a distant colleague of yours, but I just remembered what I think was the most stupid question Jason ever asked me, Dr. Seligman. One day, after I had settled down into that delicate chair without a headrest that he thought appropriate for his patients and before I could go off on one of my mad tangents again, he asked me whether I thought that I'd been a good child. Not whether I had been a good child, but whether I thought I had been a good child; only someone who has grown up in Britain could ask such a question, don't you think? As if your history was somehow up to you and your interpretation, like you had a say in it, like it was a happy situation. And it didn't make me angry, but I suddenly grew so envious, because I realised that not everyone had grown up like me, that you could look back at things and be joyful. That facts could be flexible. I mean, I know that as Germans we can never get away from our past and simply start growing happy flowers in our front garden—our outlook will always be something that has been raked to death and closely resembles concrete. That's just how it is, but Jason's question not only made me realise that people here think that they have agency in their past but also that they are free from the troubles of guilt. That because they won a war, they can always claim to think that they were good. And they even have a Queen, and they always make it look like they only need to build memorials for themselves and not for the crimes they have committed elsewhere. I remember when I first moved here; it was so fascinating for me that soldiers could be heroes and that all that remained of an empire that spanned the globe was a love of the exotic—of sugar, rum, and spices—and the comfort of a universally spoken language. Can you imagine what it means to someone like me to imagine the luxury of a clean past, Dr. Seligman? It must be like finding an acceptable way to fuck puppies, to sink down in endless layers of fluff and to not feel anything upsetting ever again. And I wonder if someone should tell Mr. Shimada about this, that what people really want is oblivion and fluff and not a full-on robot fuck. I don't actually remember what my reply to Jason was—I'm sure I found a way back to my usual disgraces without revealing anything too important, or maybe I pretended that I didn't remember much of my past—but now that I think about it, another story comes to mind. And even though this process has long become normal, it still makes me feel a bit funny, like I am being dishonest whilst really it's something else. Because the story I am thinking of and that I would now like to tell Jason is not my own but one of K's stories, and you might think that would qualify as a lie, but to me that's different, Dr. Seligman, because if I am honest, I cannot remember who I was before I met K.

Has that ever happened to you, Dr. Seligman, that someone has split you into two versions of yourself? Before and after. That every word you say suddenly feels a little strange because you have a vague sense that your tongue used to move in different ways before, but you have no way of knowing what they were? That you suddenly take a strange pride in your imperfections, and your movements seem to have adjusted to someone else's reality? I never used to feel this sudden sadness, and I could swear that my nose used to be straight, that there was a symmetry before that distinguished my face from those of others. And I cannot understand why my eyes are suddenly so green. It's almost like K poured some of his purple into my veins and bones, making sure that everyone could see the traces he left behind, that I belonged to him in a way that only lovers think they belong to each other. That every sound that left my body would carry the ring of his voice and every move the reluctance of his fingers, once he had satisfied his needs. And I think that in a way that's all we are: other people's stories. There is no way we can ever be ourselves. I tried for so many years to be something they call genuine, but now I know that I am not one thing but the product of all the voices I have heard and all the colours I have seen, and that everything we do causes suffering somewhere else. And in a way, it doesn't matter whose story it really is and looking back, I don't think that K and I were ever separated along those lines. I know that he wouldn't mind, that he would love for his past to be put on display, and I am sure that even you, Dr. Seligman, with your mysterious seven frames on your desk, are made up of other stories. You know, somehow, I am beginning to sense that there is another side to you, that maybe these frames don't contain pictures of your children and grandchildren, that maybe they contain your seven favourite sins. With the changing light my head is getting a little dreamy—I think I can see the first snowflakes dancing outside your window—and I am starting to feel that you are capable of more than just loving one wife. And please don't think that I would judge; if anything, I admire perversions and would love it if every morning, after having had breakfast with your wife, you come up here to masturbate to a different debauchery whilst waiting for your first patient. That this is how you've been able to smile at your wife through all these years. Or even when you are on the phone, if you ever answer it, or with a patient, you can always be charming and relaxed in the knowledge that you are not the person they think they are talking to. That their re-spectable Jewish doctor sometimes gets off on little pictures of our late Führer. Nothing would make me happier, Dr. Seligman, than if you had a different picture of a different Nazi for every day of the week, claiming what is so rightfully yours, coming onto their immovable little faces.

Anyway, the story that K told and that I would now like to tell Jason, Dr. Seligman, was a story about how as a child, K used to write letters to people he didn't like, putting his parents in the most impossible situations, because of course most of these people happened to be their friends and neighbours. Back then everyone's addresses could be found in the local phone book; things were much less private somehow. And then K would just write down all the things he found upsetting about them, and, given his talent for observation and how mean he could be, he probably didn't spare them any details. Can you imagine doing such a thing at the age of eight or nine, Dr. Seligman? I didn't even dare to undo my plaits without asking, and K just took a hammer and shattered his parents' social life, because being the child he was, he included all the things his parents had said about them. Revealing what people always pretend they don't know, that it's unusual to actually like each other and that most of our social constructions are brought about by force or advantage. I can still imagine K doing this, just taking a pen and telling it as it is, which is why it's probably for the best that he became an artist; nobody takes them seriously enough to cause a scandal. And yet I wonder why some people are born with such freedom, with the confidence to always eat the best bits first, whilst others like me need half their life and their grandfather's inheritance to articulate their most passionate desire? You have no idea how long it took me to realise that my name was not my name, Dr. Seligman, that it wasn't laziness when I didn't react to it in the nursery but that I knew something by instinct then which I later forgot. That I simply couldn't identify with that name, the name of a girl, a woman, a female, the name of someone with a vagina. That little beast that often felt like a slug between my legs. And until this day I wince when they address me as Frau or Mrs. or Miss, or even Ms. I never felt that any of those categories could describe who I really was, and I cannot wait for the day when you will have given me my beautiful cock, circumcised and all, and I can finally ask the world to call me by my real name, by the name they should have given me all those years ago. So, in a way, this is like a baptism, Dr. Seligman: you're like the priest, welcoming me back to my long-lost kingdom.

That's not at all a strange question to ask, Dr. Seligman, but I am not really angry with my parents. I mean, how were they supposed to know that they had given birth to a freak? They never had any other children, so maybe they did sense that something wasn't right, but I don't think it was a possibility they considered when they decided to have me; my mother was always far too vain for that. She was the kind of woman who never sees what's in a shop window because she's too busy checking her own reflection. She would never have considered that her child would be anything but perfect. I used to hate all that women's stuff, the big bag with all the makeup, the hairspray in the bathroom that made my lungs go sticky, the immaculate clothes that never allowed for holes or stains, the way I could never walk in a dress. And the embarrassment I felt once my vagina started bleeding. The way my mother wouldn't stop imposing her world on me, how I had to go and see a dermatologist for my spots and cover my legs in those horrible shiny tights. How I was at the same time her rival and her product, and how I was supposed to be fuckable in her stead once her own legs had grown too tired, like in a family of stray cats where someone has to do the deed to keep things going. It used to confuse me so much how she would try to parade me around in front of people, her friends and our so-called family, knowing full well that there was nothing worth parading. And the worst thing was when she used to take me shopping, Dr. Seligman, that most idiotic pursuit where people deliberately confuse means and purpose in order to get out of the house and pretend it's possible to actually buy new trousers. And you know those mothers who go shopping with their daughters, looking almost identical? Those daughters who got it all right to a dot, who barely rubbed off that first layer of slime they were born with and allowed themselves to be broken into an exact replica of their creators? They scare me when I see them now, but back then I envied them, because my mother and I always looked like a chic lady with Quasimodo on a leash beside her—or at least that's how I felt, because I never knew how to handle my hair or how to make her happy by looking like a girl in a dress. And she must have suffered from my embarrassment, from my inability to speak about what it was that was holding me back, why I didn't have a crush on any of the boys in my school and would only use deodorant when forced to. I think her imagination might have stretched to worrying that I had turned out to be a trouser-loving lesbian, because not all girls wore skirts and dresses even back then, but nothing beyond that. And I wish I had understood that, Dr. Seligman; I wish I had known that she acted out of the insecurity most women are born with, that they are so scared of their bodies that they would do anything to look and smell acceptable, that they wear those silly little socks so their feet don't smell in summer and that all the makeup my mother tried to smear on my face was a form of war paint, her way of trying to protect me from the world, because they all know what happens to those who rebel—they know that the witches' stakes are still glimmering in the background. And a lot of the upset between us was down to some unnecessary performance anxiety imposed by a world trying to keep people without cocks in their place, and I wish we had both been wiser. But now, Dr. Seligman, for the first time in my life, I feel like I am being strong, for the two of us, like I have broken free from those chains of lipstick and perfect hair and can take pride in my worn feet and the hair around my nipples. And I know that one day we will go shopping together and she will finally be proud of this body we both used to hate so much. I'm sure of it, Dr. Seligman, because recently I have found it in my heart to forgive her. And because all of this is so very lonely sometimes, I have started to wear some of her old clothes, her cardigans and scarves—I was always too fat for everything else—and I think that's a sign that I have started to miss her in that place where I should have loved so long ago. And I admire nothing more than people who have found a way to love their mothers; I think it's the biggest challenge in life, the one thing that would make the world a better place.

I think your assistant has fallen asleep, Dr. Seligman. Or do you have such exclusive opening hours that only special people get to leave a message? The phone has been ringing for ages. It almost makes me blush that you are spending so much time with me; you must be a good man, and I am sure you always kiss your wife goodbye. K wasn't really someone who liked to hold hands much, or cuddle, or any of that other affection stuff. That wasn't the kind of intimacy he sought, and for a long time I thought that he had reserved that kind of behaviour for his wife and children, that somehow it would have confused things if he had been tender with two people. And because infidelity is a matter of small movements, of those few seconds when we don't pay attention and let go of the farce life has taught us to play. I didn't really mind that distinction; I always felt like I was getting the good bits when K was spitting in my vagina instead of using lube, and the cool temperature of his saliva as he let it drip from his lips made me briefly forget how to hate my body. I simply couldn't imagine that he did the same to his wife, but I also didn't care, Dr. Seligman. You might find that hard to believe, but I never dreamt of being in her stead. I never wanted to know what he really looked like in the morning, and I was always sure of our situation and I hadn't been raised on much affection myself, so I didn't mind his coldness. But for K, it all must have meant something else. Because that day, when we were in a hotel room with no paint to signal the obvious end of our encounter, I found it strange to just start caressing him with clean fingers, and I just resorted to stroking his hair as a final gesture. Nothing more, Dr. Seligman, just a few strokes, when suddenly his body grew tense, like a wild animal contemplating

whether or not to attack, like he was measuring the
extent of his fear against the chances of leaving the
hotel room the same person he was when he went
in. Whether this would be the beginning or the end
of his freedom. And I didn't know what to do; wary
of any sudden movements, I just paused and waited
and before I could slowly remove my hand, K was
shrinking on the bed in front of me, wearing nothing but a T-shirt, I suddenly looked at the crying
child I told you about earlier. The little boy who
can't find his way out of the dark and is worn out by
his body's reactions to his fear. I don't remember
how long he cried for, but when I finally tried to
hug him, I realised that there was still too much left
for me to comfort, that my body was still so much
smaller than his, and that all I could do was to watch
him wander down those corridors from long ago,
filled with those horrors only he could see. In our
fear we all become animals, Dr. Seligman, closed off
from the comfort of a common language; we are left
alone with nothing but our instincts to defend us.
And yet I think that it was those tears that bound
K to me; it must have been such a relief for him to
finally find someone he could cry in front of, and
after that we started meeting in hotel rooms more

often. Away from the colours in his studio, he was like a child that's teaching itself to leave the house without its favourite toy.

Bodies—and I don't just mean human bodies, Dr. Seligman—remain very strange to me. I think I just never had an eye for them. I never knew how much soup would fit into a Tupperware container, and I could never tell how tall someone was or what size of jumper would be right. Instead I always perceived people's sizes based on their personality, the space they needed to express themselves. You are bound to have a much better sense for these kinds of proportions, and you must see people very differently, but I, for instance, can never imagine my father as a very big man. In my mind, his overall insignificance has attached itself to his physical reality, and the result is a tiny man who struggles to reach the buttons of his washing machine. A man raised by men who didn't teach each other how to grow. Or Jason, in my head his feet are dangling from his chair, and maybe that's part of the problem, that I can never see bodies for what they actually are. And this includes my own, because I always felt so bad about it, because it was so at odds with the world, I always thought that it was huge, like an irregularity you suddenly discover with your tongue. I always thought that my proportions were outrageous. And plus all the stupid rules that apply to women's bodies, how a naked female chest is naked whilst a naked male chest is not naked, how I would have to wear a bikini top whilst all the other boys could be topless, how I had to accept that part of my body as sexual, as something that had to be hidden. It all made it so hard for me, and I always felt like I was supposed to see something else instead of what I was actually seeing, like there was a secret choreography that everybody had been taught apart from me. And so I just stumbled along, trying to find that mysterious rhythm that united people in their desires. You see, I feel bad for saying such things about my father when I haven't even told you what I used to think about my mother, that I could never help but think of one of those birds with ridiculous plumage when I saw her, especially when I sat behind her in the car; the word *wiedehopf*—hoopoe in English, I think—would obsessively come to mind as I watched her hair castle wobble up and down on those country lanes. But I never felt bad about it. Do you think we are taught to have so much respect for our fathers because we can never be sure that they are actually our fathers? I know that now there's scientific proof, but these things take centuries to leave our minds, like rabbits who can die from fear when you lift them up because they are still scared of eagles even if they see you and eagles have long been made extinct. But then we are most passionate when we worship the things that don't exist, like race, or money, or God, or, quite simply, our fathers.

God, of course, was a man too. A father who could see everything, from whom you couldn't even hide in the toilet, and who was always angry. He probably had a penis the size of a cigarette. The kind of man who shoots lions and overtakes women in the swimming pool. It's of course much easier to be religious when you are a man, and yet I could never understand why a single woman ever went to church, or any of the other temples, Dr. Seligman, because no religion I have ever come across had anything nice to say about women. I could never understand why my mother believed in Jesus and had a secret altar with all sorts of glittering memorabilia tucked away in the corner of her bedroom. Why would she worship where they teach nothing but shame and fear, where they came up with all that crap about holy mothers and whores, where they were scared of vaginas. Because that's really what it is all about, isn't it? Apart from trying to find a way not to die, to carry on living somewhere in the clouds with all the people you never liked in the first place, it is a way of trying to keep the difference between people with and without cocks alive. And they talk of penis envy, but look at the lengths people have gone to cripple and defeat vaginas, to tell women that pleasure is not for them, that there is such a thing as being good. I mean, how many women have covered pages and pages of books with writing about cocks and the way men are supposed to dress and think and dream? How they are supposed to be some sort of fuckable mother figure with clean fingernails and plenty of tissues in their handbag. I never understood how God, who couldn't give birth, is supposed to be the source of all life—how a man could be our creator. Unless, of course, it was what we would call *arschgeburt* in German, something that your ass gave birth to. Maybe that's what this world is, Dr. Seligman: something that came out of a holy man's ass, the leftovers of broken stars and an imploding universe.

Since you are asking, Dr. Seligman. There was

actually one other thing that K told me about his childhood. He told me that he had often dreamt of hanging himself in his parents' garden. He had even picked a particular tree, and he had always known that it would have to be done in the fading light of a winter's day, never in full darkness, with a few gentle snowflakes resting on his arms and shoulders—bright and shiny against his dark coat, like the diamonds in Empress Sisi's hair. He didn't tell me why he felt that way, and it doesn't matter; there isn't always a reason why we feel a certain way. It's not always linked to some trauma, to what other people have done to us, because sometimes we are the agents of our own sadness. That's what he told me, and he wasn't crying when he did so; we weren't in a hotel room, Dr. Seligman, but on the floor of his studio, and he had taken a large brush and started to cover my entire body in purple. His chest hair dark with sweat. He had never done this before, and he was smiling whilst he did it, and even whilst he was telling me about this childhood image. I asked him why he had never tried to paint it, to render it in a place outside himself, but he just made a funny noise instead of a laugh and carried on painting my skin, his strokes so much more firm

and confident than mine, like he had an actual reason for turning me purple. The image doesn't scare
me, he said after a while, Dr. Seligman. And I only
paint the things that scare me, like dogs and rats,
confined spaces or heights. All you see on the can-
vases around you are my fears, my little Strudel—
that's what he used to call me—but that image from
my parents' garden, the tree I know so well, and all
those different shades of green and grey and brown
and my little body hanging against the beautiful
backdrop of the last light of the day, and possibly
some snow on the ground, the last warmth from my
little body visible in the cold winter air—that image
doesn't scare me. That image is my only source of
comfort, it's the only thing that I've always believed
in, the only freedom I possess. It's what allows me
to get out of bed in the morning after thinking just
an hour before that today I wouldn't be able to. I
find sleep at night in the knowledge that this image
will always be there. That this tree is still growing
branches strong enough to take a life.

It's almost like things began to shift, Dr. Seligman, when I realised what was really going on.
And maybe this all had to happen so that I would
finally understand that I had to come and see you,

that the only true comfort we can find in life is to be free from our own lies. That it was my duty to end this masquerade. I knew then that I would never be able to unsee things again, that I wasn't just thinking outside the box but that I had set the box on fire many years ago and refused to look at the lighter in my hand. I can't describe what it's like, Dr. Seligman, when you first realise what it means to look at a man free from the constraints of your own body, when you learn to see with your own eyes, when you realise that your vagina isn't real and that everything you thought you knew about desire isn't true. I don't know how flexible you are, Dr. Seligman, and what things you might have tried, but I was never able to find my way back to those other rules and aesthetics; I could never look at K the way a woman would have looked at him. The way my mother would have looked at him. And yet I tried, because with him things were different, because he sometimes allowed himself to be desired in those other ways, and because I liked to believe that he knew. That he played those games to please that other part of me, and that for as long as he would allow me to paint his skin with his beautiful colours, I would forget all about my own lies. That there were enough colours in his studio to reconcile me to my life as a woman. I really believe, Dr. Seligman, that I am not intrinsically bad, I am just rendered bad by my circumstances, by the fact that you cannot transcend your physical reality in your mind, that you cannot fuck faith alone, no matter how hard you try. That's why all religion is doomed to fail you in the end, because when you wake up at night and the only man you ever thought you could love is sleeping next to you, your bodies covered in all that you had to give to each other, the way lovers are supposed to look, and yet it all feels wrong, it all feels like you are lying and cheating, like a mermaid who is sinking her lover's ship—then you know that no disciple ever understood what it means to be in love.

Do you believe in hell, Dr. Seligman? Or do Jews only go to heaven? I don't believe in either, but it still scares me sometimes, and whoever came up with the idea of eternal suffering really must have had a sick mind. Someone with a messy soul and too many rats in their bedroom; why else would you go around telling people that the pain they had to endure during their lives was not enough? To take that last consolation away from them. And

I sometimes have those nightmares, Dr. Seligman, where I can't stop bleeding, it's very painful, a vein in my elbow has been opened and the blood keeps coming, but I don't die, and there's no way to stop the bleeding or the pain, and because I'm always so tired I never wake up. In the morning it often takes me a long time before those spectres go away. But I really like the idea of you in heaven; you certainly deserve to sit on a fluffy cloud for performing this miracle, for finally letting me escape my tree. Isn't it funny how we fear something we don't believe in? I used to feel like that about love, the idea of being tied to someone in that way used to scare me. I was always like a wild creature trying to outrun the lasso above its head, terrified of the possible comforts of captivity. I never wanted anyone to know what was really going on inside my trousers, and that's also why I had to threaten my colleague with that stapler, to signal that I wasn't ready for my cage, that I would stomp on all the flowers and biscuits he would ever dare to present to me. That one moment of excess after one of those drinks things doesn't mean that anything has changed, that anything can be claimed or that tenderness was allowed back onto the open field of our everyday. But of course a rejected man is like a boar in rut, and nothing is further from his mind than justice, he wouldn't even spare the trees, and I only picked up the stapler after he started talking about romance—a man's most dangerous weapon—and I suddenly saw wallpaper and brightly lit rooms and children, and I was so shocked that he had the audacity to see nothing but a woman in me that I told him that I would staple him to death. I am not usually that violent, Dr. Seligman, and I am sure you know how difficult it would be to actually do that. It would take a very long time, and I wouldn't exactly describe myself as very dedicated. I never last very long.

My legs are starting to feel quite tired; it's been such a long time since I spread them like this for anyone, Dr. Seligman, but I think that this new friendship of ours is remarkable in so many ways, and I never thought I could talk like this to someone I know. K and I always agreed that the only real conversations you can have in life are those with strangers at night. During the day, there is no anonymity, and if you just start talking to people, you are a freak, most likely one of those Bible weirdos, but there comes an hour every night when Jesus's

disciples are safely tucked away and the differences
don't matter anymore. For me this has always been
the only real intimacy; those were the only people I
could share things with. The people I met at the bus
stop at night, the people sitting on empty benches,
or the sad women selling sweets and cosmetics
outside the toilets of clubs and bars. Those were
the only real people I ever met in this city, where
everyone is wrapped in impenetrable layers of fear
and ambition and all our attempts at communica-
tion end in loneliness. With people that seem so
empty that they must have sucked up all the air that
was left, crippling our lungs with their meaningless
existence. But with strangers it's different; you can
be sad in front of them. Do you have that as well,
Dr. Seligman? I can never be sad in front of people I know; there is a mechanism that always allows
me to function, and you have to believe me when
I say that I usually act out of a profound sense of
sadness and despair. If we were to wait until the
soft darkness of the early morning, somewhere between three and four, you would be able to see it
shining through, Dr. Seligman—the face that is buried underneath all the jokes. And K always loved
the idea that there were a few strangers in this city

who knew it all, who knew why he sometimes cried like a child and which drawer in his life this alphabet of fear came from. That without revealing our faces and names we carry each other's secrets and guard them through the night as though they were luminaries, precious pieces that bind us together, make us recognise each other as human, in those fleeting moments that have become so rare. And as we come home from our nocturnal walks, Dr. Seligman, those secrets are glowing in our hands, fragile little creatures that we will nurture back to life. I wish K and I could have remained strangers; I wish I could call one of his secrets my own and feel it glowing next to me in the dark.

I don't remember now whether I have told you about the Baby Jesus machine. I have the terrible habit of repeating myself; it's one of my mother's many bad habits that I can't escape. I haven't mentioned it yet? So, there is a church where my grandparents used to live, and in that church there is a machine, like a vending or a gambling machine but made of glass so that you could see exactly how the transaction worked. If you put ten pfennigs into the slot, a little Baby Jesus would come out, ride around in a circle, and give you a blessing. I don't remember if Baby Jesus waved during his rides, but I remember that he had tracks, and that I always used to think how tired he must have been at the end of his shifts. Absolving all those old and young Nazis, getting paid less than the cheapest whore. And they probably had to oil him once in a while or get a mechanic in when he went on strike or got one of his limbs stuck in an indecent position. When his halo had come undone. You know, Dr. Seligman, how they say that nobody wants to do evil, that we are conditioned by our circumstances and our lack of judgment, our *unverstand*, so maybe we should forgive this Baby Jesus for blessing all these people, for not setting himself on fire or spitting out his wheels in protest every time these people fingered his little slot. For making it so simple, one quick ride, and all your sins vanished. Knowing the Catholic church, you probably didn't even have to show up and could just send someone in your stead. It probably didn't matter as long as you kept Baby Jesus moving. Absolution has always been a question of class, and so I often wondered, walking home with my mother and my grandparents, what it was like for Jesus at night, all alone in the dark church, whether he regretted his cheap love and all that universal forgiveness, whether he sometimes tried to reach over to the candles for the dead and try to wreak havoc. Thinking about it now, I don't see why he would have cared. His mother never had to fuck anyone to conceive him; as far as we know, he was happy with his cock; and he probably didn't have to pay rent. What more could you want? But back then I wasn't allowed to make jokes about him; my mother was unusually fond of the little machine and always made sure she had the right change with her when we went. And I learned to respect this devotion with the same instinct that prevents us from laughing about a helpless animal, long before my grandmother mentioned in passing that the baby in the glass box reminded my mother of that other child they'd had before me, the one that was stillborn, the one they had bought blue wallpaper for and that was buried somewhere nearby. My grandmother had reached that age when it has become unnecessary to comment on things, and I was too young to ask questions, and so we just carried on walking down the hill. The sun not yet ready to end the day.

I used to think that it didn't matter who your family was, that you could just stick any photo on your wall and be done with it. No stranger would be able to tell that you bought those relatives at a flea market, that they came with the frame and that you were just too lazy to take them out. And when my grandmother told me about my dead sibling, Dr. Seligman, I didn't care. Or, to be very honest, as we were walking down that hill, I was glad that all that remained of him was hidden inside a Baby Jesus machine inside a remote Catholic church run by those obscure Polish monks they had to start hiring at some point. I was glad that I was the only one, and as I grew older I became so jealous of this other sibling I had come to call Emil. Yet another example of hating something that didn't exist. I couldn't stop thinking about what life would be like if Emil was there, if he was sitting at the table with us, what he would look like. How beautiful he would be. For no matter how happy I was that Baby Emil was tucked away in that glass box, cared for by those strange monks, I never thought that he would be ugly. I always thought that he would be one of those slender and elegant boys, with the bluest eyes and skin that would turn golden in the sun. A face beautiful beyond all that talk of male and female, a face that the Ancient Greeks would have admired. And for many years I felt like nothing but the afterbirth, like some unhappy heap of cells put together in a hurry to resemble a person. I felt like Dr. Frankenstein's leftovers. And I have to admit that I spent many moments hating him, that I never mourned for him, and certainly never considered my mother's feelings, nor my father's, if there ever was such a thing. I even stopped visiting him; I left him to gather dust in his glass box, waiting for the first specks of rust to attack his wheels, the first crack to shake his transparent foundations. But then, you know, Dr. Seligman, how it's impossible to walk in a straight line when you are blindfolded, no matter how hard you try, you will end up doing a circle and most likely you will return to where you have started from. When I don't think of my life as a basketball that bounces off the rim and hits me in the face, I think of it as one of those blindfolded lines, as someone who always tried to walk straight because I couldn't see and no one bothered to tell me that it was impossible. That for as long as I refused to see, I would keep coming back to myself, my own mess, the catastrophe of my own pathetic existence. It's so clear to me now as I lie here, that I didn't spend so many years hating a dead baby in a glass box because I didn't want to share my food or my parents' measly affection, my father's strange attempts to bond with me over fixing things that weren't broken and my mother's desire to see her life happening on my face, her endless interference with my body, her fingers arranging my hair when I had long passed that age. I can still feel them on my skull. I would gladly have shared those awkward holidays in family resorts, their overall disappointment in my lack of fame, and the many times they tried to make me embrace physical activities. I am sure you are too old for your mother to have dragged you to a Body Attack class, Dr. Seligman, one of the many reasons you remained so dignified. But I can tell you, my struggle was real, and I was so busy, so desperate to hate my dead brother, Emil, not because I couldn't share but because I hated myself and I wanted nothing more than to be him. Not to be like him but to be him. And not because I thought that he would have gotten a better deal from my parents but because he was a boy, the boy I always wanted to be, and I was so jealous that he had been given the chance to be born with that correction, that it could be so easy and yet I had to live this miserable life instead of him. And that's why I decided to take his name, Dr. Seligman, to free him from his box and give him the chance to live some of that life he never got to see. And even though I will never be as beautiful as him, will never move with the grace of the people in between, I think it's the right thing to do. And once I am done here, I will go to that church and take him home with me. I sincerely hope that he isn't a religious artefact by now, so that I can free him from his box and his wheels and place him in one of the few sunny spots in my room, next to my flowers and my books, where he will never have to bless anyone ever again or serve as the surrogate for people's broken dreams. And I really hope that he will then forgive me for having taken so long, for not realising that my other side could be my brother, for not understanding that it takes several minds to be beautiful.

And so, you don't have to feel like a murderer, Dr. Seligman, because you are not really killing me or my vagina; you're really just making space for Emil to move in as well. That way we will share that inheritance that my mother didn't allow my father to keep after my grandfather's death last year, freeing him from the burden of being the favourite son. The inheritance that my father then gifted to me in a heap of illegible paperwork without telling her, my great-grandfather's hitherto untouched property, making me his daughter until the end of time. A dead man's favourite descendant. Because secrets are thicker than blood, I need a brother to get me through this. And so, we will take his name, because I have always hated mine and because I think that Emil deserves it after all those years of prayers and Nazis and underfucked old ladies. I really hope he didn't have to witness too many obscenities when the monks were on their own. But I wonder whether you sometimes feel like Dr. Frankenstein, Dr. Seligman; do you feel like you are creating monsters? I know that's how a lot of people feel about people like me, and I guess they are right in that we are staring in from the outside, that we see through their actions and know all about their little lies. And I think that's what makes us so ugly in their eyes; knowledge makes people ugly, which is probably why we think that stupid people are easier to fuck, or more fuckable—that they are not tainted by the obvious and, not unlike animals, much more in touch with their bodies. Officially that's of course considered to be a bad thing, at least that's what I gathered from my mother's complaints whenever

I sat with my legs apart, my inability to sit properly because I never understood why there were two different ways of sitting for people with and without cocks. And I constantly got them wrong, because I was forever confused by the fact that as a girl you actually have less to hide than a man, but that was before I understood that a cock is some sort of sword, an object of pride and comparison, whilst a vagina is something weak, something the owner can hardly be trusted with. Something that will always be a fuckee, that can be raped and get pregnant and bring shame upon a house and family. Something that needs protection without anyone ever questioning that need for protection, why it is that streets aren't safe at night and that girls with short hair look like boys and not the other way around. I always found all of that terribly confusing and often thought that maybe the cocks should be hidden instead, that we should ban the weapon and not the wound. But anyway, I think that our bodies know things long before our minds, Dr. Seligman; they will have all the words written on them long before our tongues can find them and our teeth can pull them apart in the empty space between our gums. And in some cases, words can take years to follow our bodies, to say what has already been said. K knew all about that; he had painted enough bodies to be able to read them, to understand my movements, how I could never really walk in tight shoes or be friendly in that way girls are supposed to be, and even though my body was sometimes a secret and took a little longer to show itself, he would eventually have had to see that this unicorn had more than a tail. He must have known what it meant when I stopped shaving down there, when I let my vagina be buried under that dark hair that women are not supposed to have and kept only the area around my other hole neat. He must have understood what my body was trying to say when there was suddenly hair showing around my nipples and my hands started to grab him with that new firmness, when I suddenly slapped him during our final moments of oblivion; he must have understood, don't you think, Dr. Seligman? That it wasn't my heart that let us down.

He always said that the colours came after the drowning, Dr. Seligman. The colours that K painted were the colours he saw when he closed his eyes at night, circles and lines glowing and buzzing in the dark, there and not there, always out of reach and too perfect to be the product of his imagination. The colours appeared after he almost drowned in his aunt's swimming pool as a small child, after he thought that blue, the kind of blue we all associate with a better life, the colour of the holidays we never had, of the freshness we dream about in stuffy moments, would be the last thing he ever saw. Afterwards he thought that this was the moment when he became a painter, the moment when his cousin tried to drown him by showing him life beneath the water, when K learned that violence binds us together like nothing else, and that nothing is more violent than the body of a five-year-old. It's like when you first learn the difference between being hit with a flat hand and with a fist; you will never forget it. And we all know the co-lour of a swimming pool, its smells and the taste of the water, so once again there was something quite public about K's trauma, about the ways in which life had chosen to shape him and the use he made of it. In those moments he often reminded me of those strange plants that people dump in the forest so they don't have to pay for their garden waste, those plants that clearly don't belong there and that insist on blossoming in spite of their hostile surroundings. That don't just go away because they don't belong there. K was exactly like that: he didn't care that most people didn't like him, that they found him arrogant and knew he was most likely cheating on his wife, a ridiculous artist with too much hubris and not enough talent, a spoilt kid, a bad father, and a hypocrite. He didn't care, Dr. Seligman; he simply blossomed and refused to be put down by those ordinary beasts and their ordinary colours. K always chose how to see himself, and I loved him for that. A bumblebee that didn't know that according to the laws of mechanics, he wasn't able to fly.

Do you care for hotel rooms, Dr. Seligman? I have always admired those shiny surfaces, and I think that if I had ever written a book, it would have been about hotel rooms. I just love the idea of a space where your actual life doesn't matter anymore and time has ceased to exist. They are like airports, except that you can be naked and don't need to pretend that you are a frequent flyer or that your job allows you to travel the world. Hotel rooms are much more anonymous in that way, and their bedsheets are usually crisp enough to carry a mild euphoria, and even though I missed the colours in his studio, I did enjoy meeting K in those empty spaces. It was much more like being with a stranger, and I think everyone should make use of them sometimes. Do you ever take your wife or your seven Nazis to a hotel room, Dr. Seligman? Or maybe you take both? I think you should; there is something about that confinement in the unknown that excites us in a good way, and it always gave me a hint of the kind of sex people must have had in bunkers during the war. And maybe that's what K and I were, two people trying to fuck their way out of the apocalypses they both carried within themselves, out of the fear our bodies couldn't handle alone. I sometimes think that's why people secretly long for wars—not just so they can torture their descendants with stories of mutilated bodies and having to eat potato peels but mostly so they can have actual sex again and not that tame stuff that freedom and peace have to offer. And even though we were careful to always use a different hotel, Dr. Seligman, we didn't manage to remain strangers. Thinking about it, I am sure that K actually told me where he was from but I forgot, or wanted to forget, to protect him from the inevitable. But the inevitable came, and because K could only sleep with the lights on, I cannot pretend that I didn't hear or see it happening, that he didn't say those words you shouldn't say to someone like me, to a barking cat. It's like asking someone not to die, like speaking in one of those impossible grammatical constructions. But he said it anyway, Dr. Seligman; after he opened his beautiful green eyes in the middle of the night, he said, BE WITH ME ALWAYS. And before I could say anything in reply, he had fallen asleep again, that heavy sleep that nothing can disturb. A child's sleep. And it's not that K wasn't a good man—he wasn't the kind of man you would imagine fingering a dead chicken or who would aggressively watch credits at the end of a film. The kind of man who takes pride in the smell of his own shit. He was the kind of man my mother would have welcomed in the shower, and what more could you ask for? We all just want to fuck where our parents have been, and I didn't care that he was married with children and all of that. Those things don't mean anything to me, and I hope that he knew that I hadn't suddenly become a square and that Emil would have stayed with him until the end of time, but the person he wanted had long ceased to exist. That he had been with a ghost, and like a ghost I vanished from that room whilst he was still asleep, which really feels like killing someone with their eyes shut. And when I think about it now, I always feel like I had his blood on my hands as I closed that door—not his colours, not the purple he had chosen for me, but that my fingers were wet and sticky from his blood. Like someone who had just poisoned their dog and had to leave the room because they couldn't bear to look at those eyes again. I felt like someone else's nightmare, Dr. Seligman, and I never know how long you have to stare at a wound before it stops bleeding. And yet, as I walked down that corridor in the early morning, something was different, and by the time I reached the reception area I couldn't help but smile at the first face I saw. It was then that I knew for sure that she had stayed in there with K and Emil had left with me. That we were finally safe.

Back when I was younger and still living in Germany, Dr. Seligman, I once saw a documentary about a young woman who was allergic to everything. She spent her life living in a house with very bright rooms but no windows, because she was even allergic to the sun. Her skin would go red and blister at the slightest touch of a sun ray, and so she lived like a snow queen, covered in eternal darkness, invisible to the human eye. But since she wasn't really a fairy-tale creature, and even Dr. Zhivago had to eat something in his icehouse and possibly even go to the toilet, her life was an ordeal. For even though they found white clothes to cover her skin, there was nothing she could eat without discomfort, nothing that would not make her retch and choke and swell. And like a pet whose demands on life had become intolerable, her parents sometimes thought of putting her out of her misery—or their own, depending on your point of view—until one day one of their neighbours arrived at their doorstep with a dead squirrel. A red squirrel, one of the good ones, not one of the grey squirrels we have come to think of as only slightly better than rats because they steal birdfeed and dig out flower bulbs. The neighbour wasn't young, not a possible suitor for the lonely bride, and so they accepted that he acted out of kindness. They skinned the tiny creature and threw away its bushy tail and proceeded to boil the little meat it had to give. They told her what it was, and she didn't mind; she ate, and nothing happened. Her body kept as calm as when you or I eat one of those grapes that fortune has handed to us. It was like a miracle, and unlike some of the first American settlers who died from eating nothing but rabbits, long before we were saved by our five fruit and veg a day, she happily lived on squirrel alone. The neighbour went hunting for her every day, but because her immune system was so fragile and strangers and their germs posed all sorts of risks, he never got to see her, never got beyond her doorstep where her parents received the precious spoils. And yet he carried on, and whenever the squirrel was young and tender, her tongue rejoiced, and her heart blossomed with gratitude.

I like to imagine that after a while she asked for the tails to be kept, that she decorated her room with red squirrel fluff and that, since they were the only things that she and her mysterious hunter had both touched and nothing is as sexy as a stranger, she started playing with them. Every tail was like a new encounter, the wall a map of her orgasms, shy and gentle at first until they became loud and hungry, and she started to play with several tails at the same time and felt itchy enough to fuck the wall. But this is of course just my mind wandering off, Dr. Seligman, I am sure that none of this happened and that all the tails were disposed of in the most respectable manner, and that in the end his love, by keeping her alive, did nothing but increase her suffering, whilst the other love—that of her parents—would likely have killed her before she could feel a first wrinkle on her forehead. That's probably why I like to think about this story—not so much because of the squirrel-tail masturbation but because of what it says about love and about how it really is an egoistic pursuit, how it's irresponsible to let someone fall in love with you and yet impossible to avoid. For even if you bury yourself alive in a room without windows and declare yourself allergic to the entire world, someone will find a way to put their heart under your foot. It took me so long to understand that, and anyway, how was I supposed to know that men die from broken hearts too? I always thought that was only for girls.

Do you think it snows above the sea, Dr. Seligman? It's almost dark outside now, and often when I lie awake at night and cannot sleep, I think about this image. Don't you agree that it's the perfect illustration of innocence? Those beautiful white snowflakes falling from the night sky, quietly, from heaven with its holy blue and all its celestialness, dancing in the breeze above the waves, rustling against each other with that divine lightness that only an angel's wings could imitate, just before they are swallowed by that dark sea of filth and toxic waste, a flood of dying creatures. Never to be seen again, with nothing but a split second before they are subsumed into this big mass of different layers of darkness that makes no difference between its components, its inhabitants. Where everyone and everything has to swallow the same amount of dirt and disease, day in and day out. And yet they say that they're all different, don't they, Dr. Seligman—that each snowflake has its own unique crystals, and so in many ways they are like us. Some of them fortunate enough to be born on those pretty mountaintops, in groups large enough to bury entire groups of ugly German tourists with their ugly mountaineering gear beneath them. Others land in people's front gardens, where they are put together to resemble men made from snow with a little orange carrot cock and others, like me, land in that sea of darkness with no real purpose other than to prolong and worsen our miserable existence and only a very select few get to land in those regions that reward them with eternity. Those special snowflakes that will still be here long after we both have died, Dr. Seligman. I am sure that the Snow Queen herself has filed them to perfection, that there is an intrinsic reason for their immortal glitter, that it can't just have been chance.

So, I never bothered with innocence, Dr. Seligman, and I never believed in it, because my split second was too short to make anything but a monster of me, and over the years I have become familiar with not being able to see my own hands at night, with the comfort of not having to keep my days clean. I wonder if you ever get bored or lonely on your mountaintop, Dr. Seligman? If you have a secret cave for your vices. But then, as a Jew, you will go to heaven anyway, so you don't have to worry. And when you will look down on me from your fluffy cloud surrounded by your frames, dragging my semi-automatic sex robot Martin from hotel room to hotel room, using that beautiful cock you gave me in ways you might think ill-intended, look down on me in kindness. Real kindness, not the self-involved kind of kindness Jason tried to kill me with. For he wasn't first seen on a mountaintop either, I am sure he first landed in a sewer and spent half his life licking himself clean, but if you look close enough you can always see some shit shining through from underneath his polished crystals. And I don't know about Mr. Shimada; I've never met him, and I don't know what snowflakes look like in Japan—prettier somehow, I imagine, but to have a mind like his, their tips must at some point have touched something that wasn't white. Just like K; when I think of him now, I can see all the colours of the rainbow reflected in him, shining for a brief moment before he drowns again, a little diamond illuminating the darkness he was never able to escape. And then I mourn for him, because I know that he never felt his destiny, that he always thought his crystals had been destined for those higher regions, that they had been touched by the Snow Queen and that something had gone wrong when he felt himself dissolving amongst the undiscerning waves. That somehow his life had been one big mistake and that not even his death would have made any difference, that it was all too late. That it had always been too late. I don't think anyone ever drowned as many times as K, and so I don't feel responsible for when he drowned for the last time in the crisp winter air. When he finally returned to his parents' garden and confessed his love for that tree whose branches had grown strong enough over the years to carry his lifeless body through the fading light of a winter's day. I cannot be held responsible for that, Dr. Seligman; we are not other people's destinies, and it wasn't me who planted that tree outside his window and cast that shadow over his childhood, it wasn't me who showed him how to be scared of the dark. But it's me who can still feel his colours on my skin, Dr. Seligman. I can still feel the difference between the different kinds of purple, and I wish I had known at the time that colours have histories and that purple is a colour of mourning and of sadness, and that K always covered me in his own sadness and that now I carry his grief with me, because I don't believe that you can actually wash your hands, or your skin. Something will have gotten into your system before you can reach the water, and our veins are slowly filling with each other's stories and dirt, each other's colours and screams; we carry each other's broken hearts under our skin until one day they block everything and stop the flow of our own blood, and everything bursts in one final moment of despair.

We are each other's sins, Dr. Seligman, and before you take off your gloves and I get up from this chair, before I put my trousers back on to finally look at your seven frames, before you can see my face again, I want to tell you about my great-grandfather, because I think that you should know where the money for this treatment comes from. He wasn't a famous Nazi, not one of your seven favourites, which would almost make us relatives, bound together by blood and perversions. I am not even sure he was a proper Nazi; we never met, and you can never trust your relatives' stories. All I know is that he was a stationmaster and he lived with his wife and his seven children above the station of a little town in Silesia, and because things were going well he bought a piece of land for each of his seven children to build houses on once they were grown, to live happily with their own families, with lots of children running around stealing cake from their many aunts' cupboards. But that land was never built on; they were displaced at the end of the war, and if you were to go there now, you would find a little forest in the midst of a small Polish town, home to Bambi and his friends, a piece of nature preserved from the evil clutches of civilisation. With bees and wildflowers and owls at night. Almost romantic, you might say, and if you were happy to go on a little walk, I am not exactly sure how long you would have to walk for, but before the sun sets you would reach Auschwitz, or what is left of it, the foundation of all that we are today. But my great-grandfather didn't work in Auschwitz; he was a devout man, a Catholic who abhorred the use of weapons and would have refused such a duty. He was merely a stationmaster at the last train station before Auschwitz, where the trains often waited overnight, where he made sure that there was no congestion, that everything could run smoothly and the empty trains could return unimpaired. He meant no harm, and when I think of him, Dr. Seligman, I see a little man standing on a platform, wearing some archaic uniform with a hat, almost endearing to a modern eye, looking at those trains and all the hands coming out of those undignified windows at the top, and I see snow, Dr. Seligman, snowflakes landing on their fingers, sent there by the Snow Queen, fragile moments of eternity falling from the sky like angels with their wings cut, their grace disappearing the moment their bodies meet. And I see snow landing on my great-grandfather's hat, on his shoulders, and on the ground in front of him, and I feel his feet longing for home, but there are too many hours left and the snow keeps falling just like the snowflakes outside your window. Falling to the sound of engines longing for motion, until the hands slowly become invisible to the naked eye and his feet have forgotten about the warmth they have once known. Until eventually the forests grow over all that is sacred, and their branches catch the angels before they hit the ground. Until the sun spreads her legs in surrender, and we are governed by a lifeless moon.

And now, let us turn this body into
    something else.

A moment of fire in the sky.

Let us leave this place, before it's invaded by
    clowns.

Let us be like gold, Dr. Seligman.

Let us change shape across centuries but
    never disappear.

Let us hold hands.

Let us be warriors.

Acknowledgments

Joachim for making me a French writer.

Jean and Olivier for allowing this to happen.

Heidi and Chris for turning this into an
international affair.

Tamara and Lauren for
making me feel so welcome.

Jacques, Joely, and Clare at Fitzcarraldo
for making blue my favourite colour.

Amy, Jordan, Morgan, and everyone else at Avid
Reader Press for the American dream.

Jane for the day in Brighton.

Laurence for allowing me all that space to grow.
(And the panda videos.)

T for buying unicorn stationery with me.

Tash for the piercing.

Sam for being the best glitter bitch.

Fair Miriam for all the encouragement.

Stephen for being Stephen.

Peter for proving that Germans can be fun.

Nick for being our Bear.

Paul for the flat in Berlin.

Florian for the friendship.

Derya for the conversations.

Marya for not explaining maths to me.

Matthew for over a decade of tea,
cake, and sorrows.

Rémi for the music.

Sergey for the patience.

Gatta and Myshkin for reminding me
that most objects are superfluous.

My parents for bringing me into this world.

Maurizio for everything.

About the Author

KATHARINA VOLCKMER was born in Germany in 1987. She now lives in London, where she works for a literary agency. *The Appointment* is her first novel.